Grim and Bear It

A Tessa Randolph Cozy Mystery, Volume 1

Christine Zane Thomas and Paula Lester

Published by Paula Lester and Christine Zane Thomas, 2020.

Chapter 1

It was a horrible day for escorting recently dead people to the other side. Truly nasty, with a chilly, persistent rain and a general gray haze in the air that seemed as though it had the ability to cling to a person like the muslin wrappings of a long-dead mummy.

Not that any day could be considered a great one for reaping souls, but since it was Tessa Randolph's first day on the job, she'd been hoping for sunshine and warmth. An inkling told her that reaping was neither an indoor nor outdoor job but a little bit of both. Still, she hoped the day would be mostly about paperwork.

Isn't that the norm? She was sure she'd be watching instructional videos and filling out the necessary tax forms all day. Then again, this wasn't a normal job.

Tessa's key slid from the car's ignition as if it wasn't even required. She patted the dashboard. "You don't like the wet weather either, do you, Linda?"

The 1981 Buick LeSabre didn't answer but shuddered a bit as its engine responded belatedly to the cue to stop running.

The old four-door behemoth might as well be a tank. She'd gotten away unscathed from two accidents, keeping Tessa safe too. And she couldn't be coaxed to move more than sixty miles per hour. But Tessa loved her and babied the car like an aging relative. And Linda had never left Tessa on the side of the road, unlike her last boyfriend.

Tessa's thin knit cardigan sagged over her shoulder, and she pulled it tighter around her chest. She peered at the building in front of her. It was a nondescript, squat gray brick structure with no obvious windows. The wooden sign over the front door said *Cooper's Life Insurance*. It was broken right in the center, the two halves sagging. The walkway to the front door was similarly run-down, with cracked concrete jutting up at odd angles, creating trip hazards galore. The hedges in front of the building didn't appear to have been trimmed for at least a decade, resembling jungle plants more than suburban landscaping.

Tessa bent her neck to gaze above the depressing scene. A dark cloud hung right over the building. She sighed.

It wasn't a life insurance company—that was just a ruse to keep humans away from the place, as was the atmosphere of creepy deterioration of the grounds.

For the hundredth time in the past week, Tessa wondered how, exactly, she'd gotten to this point in her life. She was starting a new job she had zero interest in doing, with a boss she'd rather shave her head and give up all her beloved purses than work for.

She ran her hands through thick black hair, mentally sending it an apology for even thinking about getting rid of it. It was truly her most favorite feature, and she identified with it, spending hours every week keeping it soft and healthy. Still, if it meant she didn't have to start the new job, Tessa may very well have sacrificed the swoon-worthy locks.

With all the reluctance of a toddler heading off to sleep for the night, Tessa grabbed the brown Burberry knockoff bag from the seat next to her, clutched it tightly to her chest, and zoomed out of the car. She raced for the building, thankful for all the years spent in dance class as she deftly avoided the broken pieces of concrete and burst into the business' lobby. The heavy door slammed behind her as Tessa stood there taking it in, dripping rainwater into a pool beneath her on the floor.

"You know, most civilized people would use an umbrella."

The sharp voice, oozing with self-righteousness, seemed to physically attack Tessa's ears. She had to fight the urge to run away—she couldn't escape to her room like she always had as a teen.

Instead, she smiled at the speaker as graciously as she could muster. "Actually, I find the rain refreshing. And a little water never made anyone melt, Mom."

Cheryl Randolph stood leaning on the doorjamb of her office, her arms crossed. She'd provided the genetics for Tessa's dark hair but kept hers in a sassy inverted bob with frosted tips. She regarded her daughter through red cat-eye glasses. Her glittering blue eyes, also the same color as Tessa's, showed no indication she was going to take it easy on her daughter. Quite the opposite.

She pursed her lips, covered with a shade of lipstick that matched her eyewear exactly, and then smirked. "You're a reaper, not a witch. So, you're right. Rain won't melt you. But it *will* ruin your makeup."

Tessa rolled her eyes. "Good thing I didn't wear makeup today."

"Or ever," her mother retorted smartly.

Tessa frowned, looking down at her feet. Her mother was the queen of the one-up. They could stand there all day trading jabs, but she knew her mom would always get in the last punch. And Cheryl was right. Contrary to what she'd said, Tessa absolutely hated rain and chilly weather. Her idea of heaven involved flip-flops, a beach chair, and a margarita.

Maybe she should have worn galoshes. Instead, she'd chosen comfort, wearing her baby blue Converse sneakers and skinny jeans. After all, her mother hadn't mentioned anything about a dress code.

Cheryl dismissed Tessa's bravado with a wave. "Come on. Let's get you started." She glanced at the Rolex on her delicate wrist. "You need to be at your first assignment in twenty minutes."

Tessa groaned. Of course, she'd already been given an assignment.

Her Chuck Taylors felt like they had tiny lead weights in them as she shuffled toward her mother's office.

The inside of the building was a stark contrast to the outside. The lobby floor was green and beige swirled marble. It was lined by six office doors in a ring. A large desk stood in the center of the wall directly across from the front door, but it was unmanned at the moment. *Well, thank goodness for small miracles.* The secretary was even more annoying than Tessa's mom.

A large sign made up of bronze metal letters hung on the wall above the desk, proclaiming the actual name of the business to be *The Final Journey Agency.*

Tessa snorted, just as she had a week earlier when she saw the name for the first time. If a human happened to get through the dismal exterior and make it inside looking for life insurance, the name wouldn't let them know what the place actually was—a reaper agency—but it would be *quite* the downer.

Until a week earlier, Tessa hadn't had any idea such places existed. She'd certainly never known her mother worked for one. She'd received quite an education about the original Grim Reaper and how, centuries earlier, overwhelmed by the boom in the world's population, he'd contracted out his duties.

Apparently, the original Grim Reaper now lived in the lap of luxury somewhere in the Caribbean while others, mere mortals magically imbued with his mystical abilities to transport souls across the veil between worlds, did all the heavy lifting for him.

The corners of Tessa's mouth twitched downward. She'd needed a change, that was for sure. When that ex-boyfriend, Frank, left her on the side of the road, she'd spent two hours soul-searching as she trudged home. And she'd decided to completely overhaul her life. Get a real career instead of continuing the waitressing job that had sapped the life force out of her for ten years.

Besides, she was pretty sure if Frank didn't want her as a girlfriend, he probably wouldn't continue to employ her at his restaurant either. What made it worse was all the overtime pay he'd promised her. She was never going to see that.

In the past, in dire circumstances such as these, she'd ask her dad for help. But that was the past. Tessa had to make the painful decision to go to her mother and ask for a loan to float her while she went back to school to become a nurse.

But Cheryl had other ideas. It turned out she'd recently been promoted and needed to train a replacement.

Tessa hadn't liked the idea of becoming a life insurance agent, but there wasn't much choice. Reluctantly, she'd gone to the agency with her mother and learned the truth.

Cheryl's office was a minimalist's dream. A glass desk, holding only a laptop, stood against the far wall, flanked by two black office chairs that looked so uncomfortable they seemed specifically designed to discourage sitting. The walls, painted a light rose color, were devoid of any pictures—not a one of Tessa or her father. Only a clock, which ticked louder than any Tessa had encountered in her life, hung on the otherwise blank canvas. Two silver metal filing cabinets and a coat rack with an umbrella and raincoat hanging on it completed the room's décor, if one decided to use that term liberally.

Tessa plopped into the chair, drawing a critical frown from her mother. But Cheryl didn't correct her posture. She went around to the other side of the desk, lowered herself gracefully into the chair, all the while maintaining her usual ramrod-straight posture. She clicked a few keys on the laptop. "You're all set."

"I'm set? I thought you said you had to perform a ceremony to grant me my abilities?" Tessa had pictured something like a sprinkling of fairy dust or an ordainment with a scythe.

"That was it." Cheryl's eyes stayed glued to her laptop screen. "You're a grim reaper. Your first assignment is out at the Sweetwater Golf Course. Mr. Dale Jeffries."

Cheryl spun the laptop around so Tessa could see the picture of a balding elderly man wearing thick-rimmed glasses. He was beaming with good-natured spirit.

Tessa scanned the paragraph below the photo to see how he was going to die and grimaced. "Harsh."

"It's not so bad, really. You'll encounter much worse." Cheryl's perfectly manicured eyebrows rose like butterflies caught on a gentle breeze. "It's not a hard job, Theresa. All you have to do is show up, and you can make a mint. It's showing up. That's the important bit."

"Tessa," she corrected, trying not to grimace at the use of her full name and to ignore the pleading tone in her mother's voice.

Sure, her mother wanted good things for her. But this was a hard job. She'd lost countless hours of sleep over it in the past week. She liked the idea of gently aiding the recently deceased on to the next point in their journey, but she wasn't anxious to be there in the final moments of their lives.

Still, she'd read the contract carefully, and it was a non-negotiable part of her job. She wouldn't get paid for any assignment if it were missed. And if it was missed, there could be dire consequences. That was where the contract was vague.

"Fine. I guess I'll head over now." Tessa rose and headed out, stopping in the doorway to launch a question over her shoulder. "Wait. Isn't that the golf course Dad liked to play so much?"

Cheryl's expression visibly softened, and she nodded. "He never shot under par, but he kept on trying." She blinked a few times as though something had gotten into her eye and then grinned. "Have a good time, The—Tessa," Cheryl corrected.

"I'll try." Tessa snatched the umbrella off the coat rack and left.

Outside, the rain had turned to a drizzle. Linda grumbled like a slumbering beast woken by a gallant knight when Tessa turned the key in the ignition. "Come on, girl. Mama needs a paycheck."

The car let out an irritated breath and then roared to life. Tessa hooted and fist-pumped. "Good girl!" she cried.

The weather began to clear up as she drove to the golf course, and Tessa even rolled down the window and turned on the radio. *I Wanna Dance with Somebody* blared from the speakers, and she sang along with abandon until she pulled into the golf club parking lot where the sun was shining.

Just like her father always joked, it never rains on the golf course.

Managing to slide past the front desk workers, Tessa went through the clubhouse and emerged onto a putting green, breathing in the smell of freshly cut grass. *Ah*. This was more like it.

She glanced at her watch, frowning a little. Dale Jeffries was supposed to pass away in four minutes, but it seemed highly unlikely to occur the way the assignment had said it would, given the current weather conditions.

From the green, she scanned the course and saw a group of golfers up on the final tee. She wandered that direction and immediately recognized her target.

He saw her too and approached, grinning. "Hey, sweetheart. Can you bring me a beer and some pretzels? I'll give you a good tip." He winked, obviously thinking she was a cart girl.

Tessa narrowed her eyes at the man. She'd spent enough years waitressing and should probably be used to men taking liberties—talking their cutesy, degrading terms and giving thinly veiled orders. But she wasn't. She still wanted to deck every guy who did it, including this one.

But it wasn't necessary to put Dale in his place. Anyway, she'd soon be delivering him to a new plane of existence. Then maybe he'd learn.

"I'm all out of pretzels," she said, putting up the umbrella in her hand, gazing ruefully at him.

As though someone had flipped off a light switch, the sky suddenly darkened, only to brighten again almost immediately by a flash of lightning. The thunder followed it so closely they seemed to overlap, and a sheet of heavy rain poured down like someone had turned on a faucet. "You should get inside. The lightning's close."

She knew it was probably against the rules for her to say such a thing. Dale Jeffries was her mark, and saying anything that may cause him to avoid his scheduled death had to be forbidden.

It didn't matter, though. Dale just shook his head, sending rain droplets spraying all over the place. "Bah," he scoffed. "I'm having the best round of my life. There's no way I'm going in now. One more shot. Then, even if I two-putt, I'll win."

The other three men in his party hurried past, racing for the clubhouse, but Dale turned back to the cart, searching for the club he wanted. Finding it, he held it over his head in triumph.

He never saw the lightning strike coming, and when Dale's soul emerged from his body, it looked hopping mad. "What? Now? *Now* is when I die? When I was going to hit under eighty!" He shook both transparent fists in the air and raged at the storm in the sky. "Why?"

His angry cry ended on a sob, and he covered his face.

"I'm sorry," Tessa said. She meant it. Sort of. "But it's time to go. I have to take you over now."

Dale peered at her between his fingers. "I'm going to heaven with a cart girl?"

"No," she snapped. "You're being escorted to the other side of the veil by a professional reaper. That's me. Now, let's go. My socks and shoes are soaked. And this caps one of the worst weeks of my life."

"Life," Dale said sadly. "At least you've still got one."

Chapter 2

Tessa groaned as she shuffled through envelopes she'd pulled out of the tiny metal cubbyhole marked 114. All three were bills. Of course. But really, what was she expecting? A check from Frank for all her back pay and overtime?

She snorted. He'd made it pretty clear they were finished. And that he was done dealing with her.

She stared at the empty mailbox, part of a long bank of them in the small room attached to the Mist River Manor lobby, thinking it would've been nice to see a rebate flyer. Or maybe a coupon for a few bucks off a pizza. This was what it came down to—wishing for junk mail. For anything except multiple demands for money she didn't have.

Tessa sighed and stuffed the envelopes into her purse. She took a second to caress the soft material. At least she still had her knock-offs. And a new job that should help her get caught up quickly.

She squeezed the bag to her side like a child might hug a favorite stuffed animal for comfort and turned away from the bank of mailboxes, gasping as she found herself face-to-face with a man.

"Oh! Sorry, Mr. Sanborn. I didn't see you there." Tessa shrunk backward. She pulled the bag in front of her, close to her chest, as though it could somehow create more space between the two of them. Chet Sanborn was inside her bubble, and he was in the way.

Sanborn lived directly above Tessa, on the second floor. She saw him around sometimes but did her level best to avoid him. He was an unpleasant man who always managed to make Tessa's skin crawl with his ogling. And if his leering eyes weren't enough, sometimes he added lewd comments to the mix.

He waved away her apology. "Call me Chet."

He said that every time they had an interaction. Tessa never complied. Somehow, using his last name felt like keeping him at figurative arm's length. *If only he was at literal arm's length right now.*

Sanborn leaned in, closer to both his mailbox and Tessa. "And being run into by you would be no hardship, ma'am." He grinned. "I'll tell you that."

Sanborn hitched up his gray polyester shorts. The waistband was being sorely tested by his ample middle section. The orange tank top was similarly strained and couldn't quite manage its job of covering the bottom of his furry abdomen.

Tessa tried to ease backward, but her spine hit the metal boxes. She was trapped. She forced a smile. "That's . . . kind of you."

Her eyes darted around the man, searching for a way to escape without seeming rude. But if worse came to worst and their interaction lasted more than another minute—she'd have no problem resorting to rudeness.

Sanborn rubbed a hand through the twenty or thirty strands of hair on top of his head and then scratched a patch of the salt-and-pepper ring just above his right ear.

He got closer, his key out to open the mailbox above hers. It was now or never. Tessa ducked under his outstretched arm, shuddering. She'd definitely felt a spritz of moisture from the man's hairy underarm. He didn't have the type of physique to pull off a tank top.

"See ya." It was both a farewell and a way of life.

She was almost out of the room and away when Sanborn spoke again. He didn't seem to find her clumsy escape act remotely unusual or a signal that the conversation should be over.

"Aren't you usually at work this time o' day?"

Tessa spun on her heels. Sanborn's question acted like a physical barrier that kept her from sprinting away. "I have a new job now, so my hours will be different than they were at the restaurant."

"Oh, yeah?" He glanced at her as he pulled open the door to his box. "What's your new gig?"

It took her brain a moment to remember what she was supposed to say in such a circumstance. "Uh . . . I'm at a life insurance company."

She took another step to the side, preparing to sprint across the lobby. She prepped her getaway to the door leading to her apartment's hallway. But before she could move, an obstacle stepped in the way. Silas St. Onge.

Great.

Tessa wanted to talk to Silas less than she did Sanborn.

Okay, that wasn't quite true. Under normal circumstances, spending five minutes in conversation with her hot landlord wouldn't cause her the least bit of inconvenience. It would give her a chance to watch for the adorable dimple in his right cheek and study the cute mop of sandy blond hair that loved to flop over his eye.

She shook her head to clear those naughty thoughts. These weren't normal circumstances. It was a horrible time to run into Silas.

Sanborn had said something, but Tessa had totally missed it. She didn't want him to back up and repeat it, either, so she did the first thing that came to mind. She laughed like he'd told her a joke she found hilarious.

The confusion that raced across his face confirmed she'd chosen the wrong reaction. *Oh, well. Too late to turn back now.*

Tessa kept an eye on Silas and hoped he'd continue talking to Mrs. Cross, the elderly resident of apartment 130.

"Have a good day!" she called to Sanborn. Then Tessa power-walked across the lobby to the door leading to the back courtyard, ignoring Sanborn's voice behind her.

She didn't stop moving when the fresh air hit her but hurried across the brick walk to a side door. She pushed through the heavy metal door into the hallway and chuckled with relief. That had been a close one.

Tessa started toward her door, moving more slowly while she dug in the purse for keys. But just as her fingers grazed metal, the door at the opposite end of the hallway popped open, and Silas strode through.

Oh, no! She increased her speed, pulling out the keys. Silas' long strides delivered him to 114 before Tessa could get there. He blocked her way. "Tessa." He grinned. "I'm glad I caught you."

"Yeah. Hi. Um, I don't have a lot of time to talk right now." She ignored the dimple and how it made her feel.

"This will just take a second."

The amount of time it took wasn't the problem. She knew exactly what he was going to say.

"You're a few days late on your rent." Silas shook his head, looking apologetic.

Tessa watched the hair flop over his eye. *Focus! Stop being distracted by his adorableness.* It was hard, though. Not only was Silas pretty much the most gorgeous guy she'd ever seen, but he also seemed to have no idea. Unfortunately for her, that made him even more attractive.

"Yeah. I know," she said. "I'm really sorry. It's just . . . I lost my job. But I got a new one," she hurried to say before Silas could react. "And I'll have the money to you by the end of the week. I swear."

Tessa held her breath. She hoped he went for it. It wasn't like Silas owned the building. He was sort of a property manager extraordinaire—the guy who handled everything from maintenance to rent collection. He also happened to be kind of a pushover. Tessa had no idea how he managed to keep the place's owners off his back because she couldn't be the only resident who constantly needed extra time to pay. Still, she lived in fear that one day, and maybe this was that day, he'd say no when she begged for extra time.

"Okay." He sighed. "That'll work. But Friday is the very last day I can stretch it for you."

"I'll have it for you then for sure."

Silas moved away from the door a few steps but then stopped and turned back toward her. Though he'd sounded like a softy before, his tone suddenly turned authoritative. "By the way. That cat you don't own was peering out your window today when I went past. You know the pet fee is another hundred per month."

Maybe Silas wasn't as much of a pushover as she'd thought.

Ugh. Pepper knew better than to hang out in the window during the day. Tessa was going to have to have a firm discussion with the black cat. Maybe if she withheld those soft salmon-flavored treats for a few days, the naughty kitty would learn Tessa meant business.

Lie. Lie. Lie. Tessa's brain caught up to the conversation. "She's actually Frank's cat. I'm just watching her for a few days."

Silas' eyebrows rose. "I thought you and Frank broke up."

Tessa winced. *How did he know that?*

Oh, right. Mist River was the world's smallest town—with the biggest grapevine made up of a network of elderly folk who treated gossiping like a job. In fact, Tessa would bet money that Mrs. Cross had been telling Silas about the breakup in the lobby just a few minutes earlier.

"Um." *Brilliant, Tessa.*

Silas waved a hand. "Whatever. Just get me the check by Friday. And do something about the cat."

As she let herself into the apartment at last, Tessa's chest felt heavy. She dropped her purse on the ratty blue couch that was a hand-me-down from her mother.

"Pepper." She made high-pitched kitty calls. "We need to have a talk, missy! Get your furry behind out here."

But the place was silent. The cat had probably heard the discussion in the hallway and knew making herself scarce was the best idea. Cats are smart that way.

The apartment was tiny but clean. And thanks to Silas, everything was in good working order. The kitchen had cream-colored linoleum flooring and a matching counter, barely enough to hold a cutting board at only two-feet long. There was no dishwasher, but Tessa mainly used paper plates anyway. When she cooked.

She opened the refrigerator, surveyed the contents, and sighed. There were three half-used cans of cat food with plastic lids, half a jar of mayonnaise, and some sliced cheese. She pulled out the cheese and opened a cupboard, fist-pumping when she found a sleeve of crackers. It was her lucky night.

Ten minutes later, she settled onto the couch with her favorite purple crocheted blanket, a plate of cheese and crackers, and a glass of wine. Thank goodness for Two Buck Chuck.

She used the remote to turn on the TV and navigated to the streaming service, holding her breath like she always did, waiting to see if the WiFi would work. She shared it with her friend, Abigail, who lived in the apartment next door, and sometimes, it couldn't keep up with both of them needing to watch rom-coms at the same time.

The service fired right up. Abi must be sleeping already. Or maybe she had a date. Unlike Tessa. Who was single, broke, and not at all in control of her life.

Loud footfalls overhead made Tessa glare at the ceiling. How could someone as icky as Sanborn have guests as often as he did?

Tessa kicked out a leg toward the coffee table when Pepper's head popped up beside it. The cat balanced on her hind legs, looking wary, as though expecting her owner to shoo her away. But Tessa shook her head and patted the cushion next to her. "Come on up, you little brat."

Pepper accepted the invitation, curling into a tight ball next to Tessa's hip. She smiled for probably the first time that day.

"You're going to have to get a job, you know," she told Pepper as she stroked her soft fur. "You can't expect my new gig to cover an extra hundred bucks a month for you to look out a window. What is there to look at anyway? An empty pool?"

Pepper seemed unconcerned, tiny snuffles emitting from her nose as she snore-purred.

Tessa chuckled. If only her life was as easy as the cat's. She snuggled down into the comfortable couch. As the movie's opening credits popped up on the screen, she thought about her first assignment and hoped Dale was settling into his afterlife. And she hoped she could settle into the routine of sending people there.

Chapter 3

The next day, with the sunshine pouring through the windows, Tessa got ready a lot faster than usual. She was almost looking forward to the grim tasks of the day. She realized that it was all a matter of perspective. Everyone and everything had an expiration date, and that was something out of her control.

As she crossed the courtyard, she glanced at the complex's swimming pool. It glittered in the sun's rays. An optical illusion. If only it was warm enough to consider a dip after work. She knew Silas worked hard to remove the leaves every afternoon, keeping the pool in tip-top shape for its eventual opening later in the spring.

Tessa wore a thick sweater against the chill. She was happy to be able to wear her cute purple sunglasses against the glare.

Linda's engine turned over immediately and purred all the way to the Last Journey office. Tessa glanced at the clock in the dash. *Ha*! She was a full five minutes early.

She strode carefully over the dilapidated sidewalk, allowing herself to feel a moment of smugness. Her mother had clearly thought Tessa couldn't handle the job—especially the being on time part. It felt good to prove Cheryl wrong.

The lot was missing Cheryl's fancy silver Audi. For once, Tessa had managed to arrive before her mom.

The lobby was deserted. Tessa made her way to the closet-sized office her mother had said was hers and booted up the laptop. It took her a couple minutes to remember how to get into the system to check her assignments.

Tessa remembered something as she watched the rolling ball on the screen do its thing while the computer slowly came to life. It was something Cheryl had said about forwarding messages to her email because the assignments went out at midnight each night. In fact, her mother had insisted she do it right then and there. But Tessa had convinced her not to worry, insisting she was competent and would do it before she left work.

Of course, she'd forgotten.

A whisper of worry slithered into her mind. "Come on," she muttered, tapping her fingernails on the tarnished metal desk.

The ball stopped rolling and an assignment popped up. Tessa gasped. Her stomach twisted into a knot.

There on the screen, seeming to ogle at her as usual, was Chet Sanborn. She scanned the short paragraph under his picture, but it wasn't right. It had the time of death, but where it was supposed to give the cause, it said *unforeseen*.

Tessa noted the time. Nine-thirty in the morning. Well, at least she wouldn't be late. Then she glanced at the computer's clock and sputtered. It was already nine-fifteen.

"What?"

The truth slammed into her. Linda's clock must be off. And every time Tessa tried to change it, she couldn't figure out how. *Ancient cars with their archaic problems, including non-self-changing clocks.*

Tessa jumped from the chair and immediately doubled over as a stab of pain shot through her knee. She'd banged her leg on the desk in her haste. She fought the urge to let out a few curses.

Hopping toward the doorway, Tessa lost her balance and crashed into the doorframe. Another jolt of pain—this one went through her shoulder.

"Argh," she cried as tears sprang to her eyes. She had to take a few seconds to breathe, waiting for the worst of the pain to subside before she could continue.

She made for Linda as fast as her bruised body would allow, making quick calculations in her head. She should have just enough time. Her apartment complex wasn't that far away.

If she didn't, the "company" probably wouldn't pay her for the assignment. And that meant she may not have enough money to cover the rent she'd promised Silas by Friday.

When she got to the car, Tessa grabbed the handle and yanked. It didn't budge. Her fingers skidded along the metal. She yelped as two of her nails bent backward. That was more than she could take. She let a swear word fly. Then she fumbled for the car's key.

Behind her, a car door slammed. Tessa hoped it wasn't Cheryl, there to see her quick fall from grace. She would for sure remind her errant kid she should've forwarded those emails. If she had, she wouldn't have had to go into the office at all. She could've waited at her apartment complex for Sanborn to pass.

Tessa spun on her heels, ready for the worst. But it wasn't Cheryl. Instead, a lovely woman, about Tessa's age, with dark skin and almond-shaped eyes gave her a bemused look.

Tessa ducked her head in silent apology, gave a little wave, and turned back toward Linda. She finally managed to get the door open and slink into the car. Through the window, she watched the woman glide, straight-backed, into the building.

Tessa turned the key in the ignition. Nothing happened. Linda did not make a single sound.

"Oh, come on," Tessa breathed out. "Don't you do this to me. Not now, baby." She rubbed the dashboard like it was a sick puppy. Speaking in a tone one may use on an infant, Tessa begged, "Just take Mama home and I'll let you sleep for the rest of the day, okay? Deal?"

Nothing.

Losing patience, Tessa slammed a palm into the steering wheel and glared at it. It was edging closer to nine-thirty.

"I can't believe you're doing this to me right now," Tessa grumbled. "Do you want me to lose this job? You won't be getting any oil changes if I do, I can tell you that."

In fact, the first thing she was going to do with her paycheck—if she got one at all, was pay a half-dozen bills and the rent and buy some real food. Then, if there was any money left, she was going to look for a new car. But there was no way she was going to let Linda know about *that* future betrayal.

She pulled out her cell phone and stared at it for a minute, wondering if Mist River had Uber. She had no idea. Tessa didn't have a data plan on her phone—she couldn't afford it. So, she'd have to do the old-fashioned thing. Call information. She dialed 411, asked for Uber, and then listened to the woman chuckle. "Don't you have the app?"

Tessa answered through gritted teeth. "No. I don't. Is there a number?"

"I can find you a cab company. We still have a few of those." The clicking of laptop buttons came over the line and then the woman announced she found a number. "Shall I connect you?"

"Yes, please."

After a quick talk with a woman with a thick southern accent, it was clear that the soonest a cab could arrive would be twenty minutes. Tessa didn't have that kind of time. She tried the car one more time, but it still ignored her polite request to start. With a groan, she jumped out of the car and started jogging. Ten steps later, she slowed to a walk, wheezing and holding her side. Admonishing herself for being so out of shape and never getting around to doing that thing where people went from completely inactive to running marathons in six months, she decided the best she'd be able to do was power-walk.

She pushed onward. She'd wasted so much time already. The next half a mile, with her paycheck on the line, felt like an insurmountable distance.

As the building came into sight, she started feeling uncomfortable. She didn't really want to be there for Chet Sanborn's last moments. It wasn't like the guy was a friend—she'd always tried to avoid him as much as possible. But still, she knew him personally. The thought of watching him die gave her the heebie-jeebies. And, she had to admit, it gave her a stab of sadness. Just because she didn't like talking to the man didn't mean she wanted him to die.

Tessa glanced at her phone to check the time as she arrived in front of the apartment building. Nine forty-five. She was super late. The only thing she could hope for now was that Mr. Sanborn's soul was still hanging around his body. The poor guy had been there alone for fifteen minutes.

She hurried across the lobby to the stairwell and sprinted up the steps to the second floor. There, she had to pause and drag in some breaths again before heading down to Chet Sanborn's apartment.

Upon arrival, she found his door was open. First, the unforeseen cause of death, now this. Her neck prickled with gooseflesh.

"Mr. Sanborn?"

There was no answer. After a few moments, Tessa crept into the apartment. The kitchen light was on, and she found a plate of sausage and eggs on the counter. The sink was piled high with dirty dishes. Tessa shuddered as her shoe stuck to the floor. *Gross.*

The plate of food didn't look touched. She whirled around and scanned the living room. No Mr. Sanborn. Just piles of clothes, newspapers, and a game of Solitaire laid out on the coffee table.

Okay, okay. Just stay calm. He's got to be around here somewhere.

She took some breaths to punctuate the self-pep-talk and forced herself through the living room and down the hall. The apartment was set up just like hers, so she knew there would be a bathroom to the left and then a bedroom at the end of the hall.

Maybe he pulled an Elvis. But the bathroom was empty. And disgusting. It didn't look like it had been cleaned in months.

Tessa threw her hand to her mouth to cover a gag. She hurried farther down the hall for a quick scan of the bedroom. Surprise, surprise. It was messy too. Still, there was no sign of Mr. Sanborn or his soul.

What in the world?

Tessa gripped her phone and considered calling her mother. She had no idea what a reaper should do when their mark wasn't where he was supposed to be. But she hesitated. The truth was, she was late to Mr. Sanborn's death. And she wasn't ready to admit that to Cheryl.

Maybe Sanborn had stumbled out of the apartment. Maybe he'd fallen down the stairs. He could be in the second stairwell—the one Tessa hadn't used when she went up.

With that idea buoying her spirits, she headed for the door. A few paces from it, she noticed the view of the courtyard through the hallway windows across from Mr. Sanborn's apartment.

Tessa stopped in her tracks. There, in the middle of the closed pool, which was covered with a tarp that held a couple feet of frigid water, was a body lying face down. She didn't know why it was such a shock. Or why she was surprised to recognize the salt-and-pepper ring of hair. She'd been looking for a body after all. But what was he doing in the pool?

Her brow wrinkled as her thoughts raced. She thought Mr. Sanborn would be in his apartment. But really, the assignment had only said Mist River Manor, so the pool was still within that description. But why would he be in the pool? And where was his soul?

She forced herself to get moving again. She needed to get downstairs. She needed to find Sanborn's spirit.

But no sooner had her foot fallen on the thin carpet of the hallway than two men emerged from the stairwell. One wore a police officer's uniform and the other was Silas. "You said the commotion was coming from up here, sir?" the cop said, his head tilted toward Silas.

"Yeah, I think it was from Chet Sanborn's apartment."

Both men stopped in their tracks, finding Tessa in their way.

"Tessa?" Silas questioned. "What were you doing in Mr. Sanborn's place?"

As though they belonged to someone else and she had no control over them, her eyes slid sideways toward the view of the pool. She dragged them back to the men as fast as she could, but it was too late. They'd both followed her gaze.

Suddenly, the cop was moving fast, coming toward her. "Put your hands up," he barked.

Chapter 4

"Come on out." The officer outside Tessa's dingy, depressing cell looked bored. He swung open the metal door and waved a hand to hurry her along.

He didn't have to tell her twice. Tessa darted out of the cell before the man could change his mind.

The burly man wore a shirt a size too big. His name tag read Stewart. Tessa followed him to the lobby of Mist River's tiny police station. She stopped abruptly when she recognized the back of her mother's head.

Cheryl was chatting with the officer at the front desk.

Stewart almost ran over her. He deftly stepped to the side, allowing Tessa to collect herself. "Hold on a second. I'll get your personal belongings out of the locker."

"Did *she* post my bail?"

Stewart shook his head. "You've been released with no charges. Your boss just let us know you were at the victim's apartment to do a physical exam for the life insurance company you work for."

"She did?"

"Maybe next time," he sneered, "you could mention that when you're being arrested."

Or next time she could think better on her feet. Tessa was sure there'd been some instructions in the computer training about how to get in and out of a location without being seen. And she was also positive Cheryl was going to tell her exactly what those instructions were. She sighed. Active learning wasn't Tessa's strong suit. She learned by doing. And so far, all she'd learned was what *not* to do.

Tessa watched Stewart disappear through a door and wondered about what he'd said. He'd called Chet Sanborn a victim. *Does that mean he was killed? Murdered?*

He'd seemed harmless, if annoying and slightly creepy. *Why would someone want to kill him?*

Then a thought flitted through her mind. Often, she'd heard a commotion going on above her in Mr. Sanborn's apartment. And during the wee hours of the morning, she'd sometimes wake up to the sound of loud voices and feet.

Cheryl glanced over her shoulder, noticed Tessa, and frowned momentarily before turning back to her conversation.

Fantastic. As though this morning hadn't gone badly enough, now she was going to have to deal with her mother's attitude.

Officer Stewart returned. "You're free to go. But we may call you in for questioning as the investigation continues." He handed Tessa her purse. "I heard this is basically your first day. Seems like maybe the job's not going to work out for you so well, eh?"

Tessa rolled her eyes. "It hasn't been the smoothest first day in the world. I'll give you that."

"A bad case of wrong place, wrong time." He snorted like it was a hilarious joke. "I guess Mr. Sanborn's day was worse. Getting strangled and thrown in a pool like that—it'll ruin your day fast."

"He was strangled?" Tessa's mind raced.

"Yep. Somebody wanted him dead real bad. A lot of somebodies, actually, from what I understand."

She raised her eyebrows. "Chet Sanborn had a lot of enemies?"

The officer glanced at the other cop talking to Cheryl. "Forget I said that, okay? Just stay out of trouble, Miss Randolph. And answer your phone if our department calls." He spun around and stalked away.

Taking a deep breath, Tessa gathered her courage. Chet Sanborn was the police's problem now. She had her own, more scary, thing to deal with. Her boss.

Sure enough, when Cheryl turned around, she shot a Level Four glare at Tessa, pressing her lips together tightly. She wore a lovely shade of light brown lipstick, and for a second, Tessa wondered if she'd let her daughter borrow it. But she quickly shrugged off that thought. Tessa had a feeling her mom wasn't in the sharing mood, unless she counted sharing her frustrations. Cheryl surely had many of those.

Tessa's mother marched out the door without saying a word. Tessa shuffled reluctantly behind her.

"Mom." Tessa felt like a kid trying to get her mother's attention.

"You're fired," Cheryl shot back, her arms crossed as she stood next to the Audi. "Just as soon as I can find a replacement, you're out."

Panic flooded Tessa's system. She pictured Silas kicking her out when she didn't have the rent on Friday. Her next thought was Pepper. The poor cat would be homeless. And she was a horrible mouser. She'd starve to death quickly on the streets. So would Tessa. She didn't have what it takes to sleep one night outdoors.

Actually, now that she thought on it, Pepper would probably just target some unsuspecting passerby with her sweet, furry feline sad-eyed expression. She'd find herself a new home by the end of the first day. Tessa wasn't likely to be so lucky.

She imagined herself pleading with Frank to get her waitressing job back. The panic the thought induced came through in her tone. "Please don't do this! Mom, I'm sorry I was late this morning. It was my stupid car. The clock in it is wrong. Then it wouldn't start."

Tessa held up a hand when Cheryl opened her mouth. "I know, I know. I was supposed to forward the assignments to my email, and I didn't. But I will. I will now. I'll do whatever I have to do. This will never, ever happen again."

With that, her speech stumbled to a halt. She tried to channel the look Pepper gave her when the cat wanted some canned food. It was pretty irresistible, at least when it came to getting some salmon pate.

Cheryl's jaw cocked as she studied her daughter.

The silence stretched out.

Tessa shifted her weight under the uncomfortable gaze. One of them was going to have to give. It couldn't be her.

She had a flashback to the time she'd snuck out to go joy riding with her girlfriends and found her mom up waiting for her when she got home. Cheryl had given Tessa the exact same silent glare while considering what punishment to dole out.

Tessa winced at the memory. Not only had she been grounded, but she'd also had her newly earned driving privileges revoked for a full sixty days. It had really set her back socially. In fact, it was probably why she hadn't been crowned homecoming queen.

Okay, that last bit wasn't quite true. Tessa was never part of the in-crowd. And she couldn't blame her mother's harsh punishment for the lack of votes. But being grounded for sure cost her the debate team presidency. She'd had to miss a bunch of meets. Then Christy Morgan had gotten all cozy with Brett Smith, Tessa's big crush. The two of them had joined forces, won the state debate championship, earned college scholarships, and eventually gotten married. Last Tessa heard, they were both lawyers in LA, living the high life.

Suffice to say, just the thought of a punishment as severe as that being doled sent Tessa spiraling down a dark path.

But what was the new job's equivalent to being grounded for a month? Anything was better than being fired.

"Mom, please," she finally squeaked.

"Fine," Cheryl snapped. "I'll give you one more chance. But just one." She opened the car door. "I suppose you need a ride."

With a sigh of relief, Tessa darted around the car and hopped into the passenger seat before Cheryl could change her mind. When her mother climbed in, Tessa said, "Thank you. I won't be late again. I promise."

"I certainly hope not." Cheryl didn't sound convinced and Tessa tried not to take offense at the sub-par confidence level. "We'll talk about what's next for Chet Sanborn first thing in the morning." Cheryl glanced over her shoulder to back out of the parking spot. "And I mean *first* thing. Don't you dare be late. You know, I think you may need a new car."

Tessa knew that was true. "I won't be late," she promised.

But something wasn't sitting right. Every time Tessa thought about her apartment, a sinking feeling whooshed down to the pit of her stomach.

"Um, Mom? I have a favor to ask you."

"I thought I just did you a favor."

Tessa winced. She didn't want to say the next words but couldn't think of an alternative. "Can I stay at your place tonight?"

Cheryl glanced over, but Tessa couldn't read her expression through the dark glasses she'd donned. "Why?"

"I can't stay at my place," Tessa whined. "There's a killer on the loose."

Her mother's cackle surprised Tessa. It made her jump toward the window. "We have bigger problems than a killer on the loose, Theresa Randolph." Her mom slapped her palm against the steering wheel. "We've got a *soul* on the loose. And your apartment complex is as good a place as any to start looking for it."

Chapter 5

Luckily, Tessa wasn't the only one creeped out about the murder at the apartment complex. Shortly after her return, there was a knock at the door. The familiar "Shave and a Haircut" of her neighbor.

"I come bearing a gift," Abi said through the door.

Tessa opened it wide to see her friend standing on the front mat with two pints of ice cream—one in each hand. She was already in her PJs—plaid pants a size too big with the drawstring cinched at the waist and an oversize Foo Fighters T-shirt from a concert they'd both attended a few years before. Abi's red hair was pulled back into a ponytail and her glasses obscured her green eyes.

"Chunky Monkey or Half Baked?" She held them both for Tessa to see.

"Am I terrible for wanting both?"

Abi shook her head. "I'm game as long as you have clean bowls."

Tessa smiled. "I guess Half Baked will have to do."

They folded onto either side of the couch, and Tessa turned on Netflix to the last episode of the *Gilmore Girls* they'd watched together. It was a lot easier than picking out something new. And the TV would just be drowned out by conversation anyway.

"I'm guessing you heard." Tessa allowed a bite of ice cream to melt in her mouth.

"Honestly, I'm surprised it took you this long to off him. That man was a creeper. I just can't believe you were dumb enough to get arrested."

"You know I didn't do it."

"But if you did, I could help you. Do you know how many true crime docs I've watched?"

"We share a Netflix account, so yes. I do. Who told you I was arrested?"

"Mrs. Cross. She told anyone who went by her doorway. She just crouched there or something, waiting to spring out. Not the best thing to do to people when there's a killer on the loose."

"Ah, but she didn't think the killer was still on the loose."

"Oh, she knows you didn't kill him," Abi scoffed. "She just needed people to talk to today. I mean, I can't blame her. Death is so creepy. One minute you're here, checking out every woman with a pulse and the next . . ."

"Yeah, it is weird." Tessa sighed. She couldn't really talk about her new job anyway, but Abi's stance on the matter made it even more difficult. How was she going to keep being a reaper a secret from her best friend? Her *only* friend aside from Pepper—and she wasn't sure the cat counted.

"Did Mrs. Cross have any idea who really did it?" Tessa asked. After a hurried search of the building, she'd resigned herself to the fact that Chet Sanborn's spirit was nowhere to be found. She kind of hoped he was off haunting whoever did this to him rather than using his powers as a Peeping Tom. The thought made her shudder.

"Of course not." Abi dipped a spoon into the Chunky Monkey. "But we know they didn't live here."

"Yeah? How do we know that?"

"Because everyone here has reverence for the pool. It's the one amenity we all agree on."

Tessa nodded, conceding Abi's point. She wondered who would kill Sanborn in such an open space and why. But she was thankful it wasn't her job to find out.

***

Cheryl made it clear she was irritated about having to stop by Mist River Manor the next morning. Tessa got back in the Audi, greeted by the long-suffering expression on her mother's face. "Are you ready to work now?"

With a bright smile, Tessa said, "Yep! I'm completely ready to grim reaper my way through Wednesday. I didn't see any assignments in my email yet, though."

Cheryl glanced in the rearview mirror and narrowed her eyes. "Your assignments are on hold until we find your last mark's spirit. Honestly, why do people have to tailgate?" She tapped the brakes. "I'm here. And this is a forty-five mile-per-hour zone. Jerk."

"Okay." Tessa brushed aside her mother's bad driving. "So, I have to find Mr. Sanborn's spirit. That shouldn't take long. Should it?"

"It had better not take more than a few days." Cheryl's tone was sharp. "Otherwise, the repercussions will be severe."

"Rep . . . repercussions? You mean, like, I'll get fired?"

Cheryl chuckled, but it wasn't a cheerful sound. "Not having a job will be the least of your worries if you don't fix this. The business of escorting souls across the veil is serious.

Losing someone's spirit so it's free to wander loose on this plane instead of crossing over—well, it's the worst thing a reaper can let happen. It may cause a chasm to open between our world and the nether." Her tone was ominous, like the announcer on a wildlife show talking about the imminent extinction of a species.

"Chasm?" Tessa asked. "You mean, like demons coming through to feast on humans? Or like the undead? Zombies?"

Cheryl rolled her eyes. She pulled into the agency's parking lot. She shut off the car and turned toward Tessa. "How would you like it if you were home from the grocery store and, suddenly, you took a step that landed you in a different place? And not just from the store to your house or the beach. Not this plane at all but the next one. Just like that—your spirit ripped through to the other side before its time. And then think about that happening to thousands of people on our side, while thousands more who have already crossed suddenly find themselves on the side of the living. Of course, they don't have bodies anymore, so they're all riled up and ready to find a human form to inhabit."

"I said zombies." For the first time, Tessa noticed her mother's coloring wasn't normal. She was pale. The usually unflappable woman was afraid—actually afraid. A chill ran down Tessa's spine. She shuddered. "Okay. That does sound . . . bad."

Cheryl set her jaw. "As reapers, we are the first line of defense against the chaos that would ensue if the living and the dead could co-mingle. Losing Chet Sanborn's spirit could trigger a dark time like this world has never known."

She got out of the car and slammed the door, leaving her words to reverberate through the enclosed space like a threatening echo.

Tessa contemplated what it all meant. Had she been aware of the consequences—of what this job really entailed—she probably would've stuck to waitressing. Serving a hamburger never triggered an apocalypse. But she'd already gotten herself mixed up with it. There was no turning back now.

She got out of the car and trudged after her mother. When she finally got inside, Cheryl was talking to someone in the lobby. It was the lovely, ebony-skinned woman Tessa had seen in the agency's parking lot the day before. The one who'd heard Tessa swear when she damaged her nails on Linda's door handle. This woman was the epitome of grace, with a straight spine, long neck, and gentle movements. She glanced Tessa's direction, revealing makeup that looked like it had been applied by a professional—subtle yet stunning. It enhanced the almond shape of her eyes and full lips.

Feeling awkward, Tessa started toward the closet-sized space she'd been assigned. But her mother's sharp voice stopped her. "Tessa. I think you should go on Gloria's next assignment with her. You won't be given another one until the Sanborn situation is resolved, which I have a conference call about this morning with the higher-ups. I don't need you sitting around doing nothing. You may as well learn something."

Gloria winked an eyelid expertly coated in sparkly mauve shadow. "Yeah, girl. Come with me. I'll show you how it's done."

Gloria's car started without issue, causing Tessa to feel a jolt of jealously. It would really be nice to have a car that started every time you turned the key in the ignition.

Tessa pushed uncharitable thoughts about Linda away, irrationally afraid that the car would hear her and act even more stubborn.

She wanted to chitchat with Gloria—ask her where she bought her makeup. But they weren't really on good footing just yet. So, she settled on talking about work. "Who's the mark?"

"His name's James Parsons. Car accident." Gloria shook her head. "He's been a heavy drinker for years and had a lot of near misses. That ends this morning. He's been drinking all night. Should've just slept in the truck for a while instead of trying to get home."

"That's not good."

"At least he isn't taking anyone with him." She glanced at Tessa, who kept her eyes on the scenery outside. "Word is you had a rotten first day."

"It could have been better, that's for sure. I lost a soul."

Gloria pulled the car onto a wide spot on the shoulder. She got out and leaned against the hood. Tessa followed her, looking around. "This is where it's going to happen?"

The lovely reaper nodded. "Yep. James isn't going to be able to make that turn." She gestured toward the hairpin curve in the road they faced before glancing at her watch. "We're about five minutes early. Perfect timing." She shot an apologetic look at Tessa. "Sorry. I didn't mean to—"

"I get it," Tessa replied. "I need to watch the time better. Don't worry. I'm not going to be late for an assignment ever again. Not only would it be risking my job, which I have no business doing right now—because I'd rapidly become homeless—but apparently it also risks causing a tear in the universe or something crazy like that."

"Is that what Cheryl said? Spirit apocalypse?"

"Basically, yeah."

Gloria snorted. "I know she's your mom and all, but I gotta tell ya—she can be a little . . . much."

The rumbling of tires drew both of their attention to the road.

In the next instant, a rusty blue pickup truck appeared, careening through the curve without taking it. James Parsons never hit the brakes. The truck soared off the road and smashed into a huge oak tree in a cacophony of tearing metal that made both reapers cover their ears.

It was immediately apparent that there was no way the driver could have lived. The front of the truck was crumpled like an accordion, pushing the bumper almost into the bed.

Gloria crossed the road and stood a foot in front of the truck, hands on her hips, watching as James' spirit rose through the broken roof of the truck. The sound of the vehicle's fluids dripping onto the ground mixed with the spirit's wails.

"Come on, now, James. You had to know you were flirting with death, driving around like that for all these years." Gloria made a clucking sound and shook her head. "Don't act shocked."

The spirit tried to focus on the reaper, but his half-transparent form seemed unsteady. "Who said that?" he slurred.

"I did." Gloria snapped her fingers a few times. "Right here. I'm your guide to the other side. So let's go."

"Other . . . what?"

"Let's go," Gloria repeated. "I haven't got all day. You're due in the spirit world."

James shook his head, and his spirit toppled that direction, upending over and over like a crazy, out of control top. Tessa crossed the road to stand next to Gloria. "His spirit is acting as drunk as his live body was. How is that possible?"

"Oh, people's spirits sometimes don't adjust to being dead for a few minutes or more," Gloria explained. Then she shouted toward the opaque figure, "James! You're dead! Let's get a move on!" She lifted a hand and waved it toward the dead man and suddenly, he stopped tumbling. He drifted toward the reapers as though held in a force field. "Sometimes you gotta take control or they'll run."

"And I guess they don't all wait around for their reaper if you aren't exactly on time," Tessa grumbled.

"Some do. Some don't," Gloria conceded. "But I'll let you in on a little secret. It's probably not quite as dire as your mom's making it out to be. She's a corporate yes-man. She's always toeing the line. And I'm not saying it's ever happened to me, but sometimes a soul just isn't quite ready to leave."

"I'm not ready!" James cried, sounding less slurred than he had initially.

"Too bad," Gloria snapped before turning back to Tessa. "Maybe your guy has a reason for sticking around. Like he wants to see his loved ones one last time at his funeral. Or . . . hey, wasn't it a murder? I know—he probably wants to see his killer caught. Hang on. I'll be right back."

Gloria used her reaper power to pull James to within a few inches of her body and, as Tessa watched, they both shimmered, growing less tangible by the second, until they winked out of sight.

Tessa crossed the road and got in Gloria's car to wait for her return, wondering whether the other reaper was right about Sanborn. Was he trying to evade crossing to the other side on purpose? All so he could see his killer behind bars. It made sense, the more she thought about it. Tessa could imagine feeling the same way in his shoes.

And Gloria had made her feel a bit better about the whole situation—unlike Cheryl. Maybe Tessa had time to find Sanborn and help him cross the veil before something crazy happened.

But how?

All of a sudden, she knew the answer. If it was true that Sanborn was staying to ensure his killer was caught, then if Tessa found the murderer, she'd find Chet Sanborn.

Chapter 6

"You know, you are way too fickle," Tessa lectured Linda. "I mean, seriously. Today, you star like it's nothing and yesterday—when I really needed you, I might add, you let me down. Listen up, old girl. You're really going to have to shape up if you expect me to keep dumping my hard-earned money into you."

Tessa pulled into the Mist River Manor parking lot, brought the car to a stop in the reserved spot for apartment 114, and shut off the engine.

In a gentler tone, she said, "You know I love you, right? That's the only reason I haven't traded you in for a newer model."

They both knew that wasn't true. There was no way Tessa could afford a new car. But she figured it was good to keep some fear of the junkyard in Linda's mind.

Grabbing the bank envelope off the passenger seat, she hopped out of the car. Cheryl had agreed to pay Tessa for the first job, the one at the golf course. Now she could pay her rent. Of course, she'd had to endure her mother's smug attitude as Cheryl wrote the check. But Tessa had decades of practice dealing with that.

Silas was in the lobby, tool bag open at his feet, replacing a chipped tile near the reception desk. *A man of many talents.*

He glanced up when Tessa's shadow fell over his work. "Oh, hey."

"I have that rent for you." She held out the envelope.

Silas looked surprised. He got to his feet, dusted off his jeans, and accepted the envelope. "Thanks."

Tessa turned to leave, already thinking about having a nice salami sandwich before heading back to work. She shuddered at the thought that reaping souls already felt like a typical job.

"Oh, by the way," Silas called after her. " A couple of guys came through here asking about you earlier. I told them I thought you were out at your new job."

Guys? What guys? Tessa wondered who would be looking for her. Could they be from the reaper agency, perhaps someone higher up than Cheryl, wanting to talk to her about the Sanborn debacle? But why? Her mother seemed to have the Tessa-lecturing firmly in hand, and Gloria had all but skirted the matter under the rug.

Tessa wracked her brain, trying to remember if she owed anyone else money but came up blank.

Then she realized who they must be.

Officer Stewart had said the police department may want to question her again. That had to be it. She trudged toward the door leading to her hallway, feeling low on energy.

As she drew near the end of the short hall before it spilled out to the longer corridor her apartment was on, Tessa heard banging. Someone was knocking hard on a door. Then, a male voice said, "Does Theresa Randolph live here?"

They banged again.

Tessa stopped short. A war was going on inside her. Part of her wanted to correct the guy . . . her name was Tessa—whatever her birth certificate said. But the rest of her wanted to stay out of sight.

However, if it was the police officers wanting to talk to her, she knew it was probably a better idea to present herself. She didn't want to get on the wrong side of the Mystic River Police Department.

But she really didn't have time. She didn't want to be questioned for hours on a subject she couldn't reveal to the police. She needed to find Chet Sanborn's spirit.

Slowly and carefully, Tessa peeked one eye around the corner. Two men stood towering over her neighbor, Mrs. Cross, who craned her neck upward and scowled at them.

"Wrong apartment," she barked. "That girl lives next door." The elderly woman jerked a thumb toward Tessa's apartment before slamming the door in the men's faces.

Tessa frowned. She didn't recognize either of them. They weren't uniformed officers, and they didn't give off the vibe of plain clothes detectives either. One looked around thirty-five and was really tall—Tessa guessed around six foot two—with reddish brown hair in a man bun, khaki linen capris, and black Birkenstocks. Definitely not a regular police-issue uniform. But why would they send undercover cops to question her about Sanborn's death?

Tessa knew the answer to that one. They wouldn't.

The other guy stood only to the first guy's shoulder. He wore black denim jeans and a black shirt with a red skull on the front. A black leather wrist cuff and boots completed the biker look. He appeared to be in his mid-fifties and had a scarred face that roughly imitated a vertical rectangle.

The first guy threw up his hands. "She's not here."

"Or she's not answering." The second guy's voice was as rough as he looked. He snickered. "We could always break in. Or are you too much of a sissy for that, Maddox?"

"I'm not a sissy, Horner."

Tessa had to bite back a giggle at the name.

"I just don't want to go to jail today," Maddox said. "So, let's go, okay?"

Tessa darted back into the lobby before the men could spot her. She had no idea who they were, but if they were considering breaking into her apartment to find her, she knew they weren't good. And she didn't want to run into them face-to-face.

She dove into the only obvious hiding spot in the room—behind the reception desk. From his spot on the floor near the tool bag, Silas gave her a puzzled look. She used her hand to make a cutting motion across her throat and then jabbed a thumb behind her, where the two men were just emerging from the hall.

Silas' face registered understanding. He jerked his gaze to the task at hand, away from Tessa.

Maddox and Horner left without saying anything to the landlord, and Tessa popped up, peering out the front window to see which vehicle they got into.

"What's going on?" Silas moved the tools behind the counter.

"Were those the guys you were talking about?"

"Yeah, why?"

"They were just banging on my door. I don't know them."

"And?"

"And they seemed to be a bit . . . questionable." She made for the glass door of the lobby. "I think I'm going to follow them."

Tessa wasn't sure when she'd made that decision, but it seemed like a solid one. She had a hunch that those guys had something to do with Mr. Sanborn's death. Of course, she had no proof. But how else was she going to find Mr. Sanborn's spirit? The pair of goons was her only lead.

"Do you think that's safe?" Silas asked. "How questionable are we talking?"

"They thought about breaking in."

"That sounds highly questionable."

"I'll be careful." Tessa jogged across the parking lot as the white Toyota Camry carrying Maddox and Horner pulled away.

She jumped into Linda and twisted the key in the ignition. The car sputtered and died, refusing to make any effort at all when Tessa tried again.

Tessa growled in frustration. "You know what? That's it. I'm getting a new car! You're going to the junkyard, missy!"

Silas, who'd followed her out, stood several feet away watching. "I think that's for the best."

"Can you drive me?"

"Are you serious?" Silas looked shocked. "Following those guys seems like a terrible idea."

"It might. But I think waiting around for them to find me again is a worse idea, don't you?"

He ran a hand through his hair, making it flop over one eye, so he had to push at it again. "I guess you're right. Come on." He crossed the lot to a shiny blue Silverado and climbed in.

Tessa ran to get in the passenger side. "Hurry! We're going to lose them."

"Hold your horses. We won't lose them." He maneuvered the truck onto the street and stepped on the gas, roaring through a stop sign at the next intersection.

Tessa scanned the area looking for the Camry and biting her lower lip. Silas' truck wasn't exactly inconspicuous. Hopefully, it wouldn't draw the goons' attention.

"There!" She pointed to the right, where she could just see the back corner of the Camry as it turned onto another street.

Silas gunned the engine, following the Camry at speed but had to ease back when they caught up too fast.

"Looks like they're heading out of town."

"Stay with them," Tessa pleaded. "I want to see where they go."

"You got it." He smirked a little, almost like he was having fun. "But I still think this is a terrible idea. If those guys are up to no good, shouldn't we call the police or something?"

Tessa imagined Officer Stewart's eye roll if she called and told him some guys were knocking on her door. "I don't have any evidence other than what I just overheard. I don't think the cops would be able to do anything with that."

Silas nodded.

"We'll just see where they go and maybe get a little more information."

"They're going to the casino."

Silas pulled into the parking lot and then found a spot at the edge of the lot. They watched Maddox and Horner get out of the Camry, which had pulled into the valet lane. Horner tossed the keys to the young attendant, who caught them awkwardly. They didn't ask for a ticket. The two headed inside.

"Thanks for the lift." Tessa hopped out of the truck and started to hurry across the lot.

"Hey!" Silas had rolled down the passenger window and leaned over to call out to her. "Are you sure you want to go in there? If those guys really were looking for you, you've essentially done their job for them."

"I'm just going to see if I can figure out who they are." But she knew Silas was right. "I'll stay out of their way," she said. "And I'll get a cab back to the apartment when I'm done." She waved and smiled cheerfully to encourage Silas along.

He frowned, uneasy to let her go. Reluctantly, he put the window up and eased out of the parking spot.

Inside, it only took Tessa a few seconds to remember why she hated casinos. They were smoky, crowded, noisy, and smelled like desperation.

She scanned the area looking for Maddox and Horner before easing into the main room. Slot machines jangled and clanged. Waitresses circulated the floor, carrying drink trays to the gamblers, most of whom, she realized, had the look of Mr. Sanborn. Chubby, bald, or both—with hairy triceps. They stared at the machines without paying attention to much else.

Tessa began to snake through the tangled path of slot machines, clearly set up to dissuade people from finding their way out. As she went, she kept an eye out for the goons. She didn't catch a glimpse of either man, but she did see a guy she knew a little from her waitressing job at Frank's restaurant. He was playing blackjack in a side room. She darted past the doorway so he wouldn't see her.

The guy was someone she'd always groaned to see coming into the restaurant. Another Chet Sanborn type. He had a horrible, ill-fitting toupee of thick black hair that swooped over his forehead. She'd watched it fall into his face a time or two when he'd slumped over the bar. He was missing a front tooth. But he put out airs like a suave gentleman, donning a fake Italian accent and making unwanted advances on all the waitresses.

What's his name again? Ricardo Vidale.

Tessa kept wandering through the crowd, and slowly it occurred to her that a lot of people were wearing tank tops like the ones Mr. Sanford always wore when he was alive. Purple, aqua, white, and orange ones that all said MRC on them. Mist River Casino.

It was all starting to make sense. Too much sense. Sanborn must've frequented the casino.

"Miss Randolph?"

The barked words made Tessa jump. She whirled around. It was Maddox and Horner.

"Um. Yes?"

How had they spotted her? Her eyes floated up to a security camera mounted near the ceiling. *Ugh!*

"Come with us, ma'am," Horner said. "Our boss would very much like to have a word."

The goon's thick hand closed around her elbow, giving Tessa no choice but to go with him. She saw Ricardo glance her direction as they passed the blackjack table. Recognition flitted across his features.

They headed for a door at the back of the small room.

For half a second, Tessa wished she was back at the restaurant dealing with misogynistic Ricardo. It had to be better than being escorted by two guys into the dark recesses of a casino where, as she understood it, she was about to be interrogated.

Chapter 7

Tessa was glad to encounter a few other people in the hallways. She'd hate to find herself alone with the odd couple who bounced insults at each other over her head like some weird monkey in the middle game.

Maddox, with his man bun coming loose and bobbing side to side, was in front. His height meant long strides Tessa had to hurry to keep up with.

"I'm just saying," he shot over his shoulder. "You're going to die of a heart attack one of these days. Plus, eating meat is gross. I've been vegan for ten years, and I'm loving it."

Behind Tessa, Horner snorted. "That explains a lot, kid. Nobody gets strong on bean sprouts and coconut milk. I imagine there's some avocado toast in your future." His rumbling chuckle was full of derision.

"At least my cholesterol is normal. And I don't have high blood pressure. You look a little red in the cheeks, there, buddy—like maybe walking down this hallway is too much work for you."

Maddox turned down another hallway and rested his hand on a doorknob, pausing to raise an eyebrow. "Don't worry. You can take a rest while we talk to Chino." His gaze cut to Tessa, and his features hardened. "Our boss wants to talk to you. Be sure you keep a respectful tone, or—"

"Or what?" Tessa said, emboldened.

"Or you're bound to dislike what happens," Horner warned.

Tessa glared at him. She held her tongue and followed Maddox through the doorway into an office three times as big as her apartment's living room.

"Wow." She stopped short and looked around. The room resembled a chic penthouse room in a fancy hotel. One wall was consumed by a huge fireplace surrounded by pale brick and set off with a mahogany mantlepiece holding a single ornate gold and black clock that looked like an antique.

Queen Anne furniture in cream, sage, and purple was prominent in the room, along with classy violet and beige carpeting that lent the space a femininity Tessa hadn't expected. The smokey air of the rest of the casino was gone. So were the sounds of slot machines, replaced by the whir of the room's ventilation system.

A middle-aged woman sat behind a desk made of some type of pale wood—maybe maple or oak—intricately carved on the edges. The word that came to mind when Tessa saw it was *delicate*.

The woman wore a pale pink suit coat over a ruffled white shirt. Auburn hair was piled high on her head, and her eyebrows had been plucked and shaped just a touch too much, leaving her looking more surprised than she probably was. The heavy-handed use of dark brow liner did nothing to relieve the odd expression.

The woman tipped her head. "You found her? That's not what you said on the phone."

"She showed up here, Ms. Chino." Horner ducked his head and folded callused hands in an obvious show of respect. "We saw her on the surveillance cameras and brought her back for you."

Ms. Chino's eyes flicked to Tessa. "I'm surprised you came here. I'd thought you'd have left the county by now."

Tessa chuckled. Maybe she'd been wrong about Ms. Chino's eyebrows. Maybe the woman was truly surprised to see her. Then her face hardened—the best it could with the bad brow job—and Tessa knew she'd made a mistake.

"Why would I leave the county? By the way, I'm Tessa Randolph." She strode forward, holding out a hand. "And you are . . .?"

Without taking Tessa's hand, the woman stood, revealing that she wore a pencil skirt that matched the suit coat and shiny beige pumps. "Melinda Chino. I manage the Mist River Casino and Hotel. And from this point on, I'll be asking the questions."

Tessa bristled. Who did this woman think she was? Not a cop. Definitely not her mother. Her tone reminded Tessa of her fourth-grade teacher, Mrs. Gatlin.

But Tessa wasn't a child anymore. She opened her mouth to put Melinda Chino in her place but caught a movement out of the corner of her eye. Maddox was shaking his head, clearly counseling her from a distance to keep her mouth shut.

Tessa stabbed a finger toward the two men. "Why were your thugs at my apartment, banging on my door and bothering my sweet old neighbor?"

Restraint was never her strong suit.

The corners of Melinda's mouth twitched downward, and Tessa got the distinct feeling she wasn't used to being challenged. The casino boss rounded the desk and leaned on its edge, crossing her ankles. She studied Tessa's face for a moment and came to a decision.

"Sanborn owed this casino money," she said.

"You can owe a casino money?"

Melinda raised one too-thin eyebrow. "If you spend enough money in this establishment, you may qualify for a line of credit. And he spent *a lot* of money here."

Horner snorted. "He spent a lot of money gambling anywhere he could. Not just the legal stuff either. He's known in all the illegal circles around town."

Melinda glared at Horner, who didn't seem to catch her point at first.

"What? I heard he knew nothing about sports. And yet . . ."

Horner finally caught on to what Melinda's hard look meant and stammered to a halt.

Melinda shifted her gaze back to Tessa. "Unfortunately, Mr. Sanborn abused his privileges with us. Ultimately, we had to cut him off. And he was delinquent in his payments." She narrowed her eyes. "Something I understand you're familiar with. Yes, we did our research on you as well."

"How much did he owe?" Tessa found herself asking.

"Something to the tune of forty thousand dollars."

Tessa let out a low whistle. She couldn't imagine gambling away that much money.

Melinda nodded toward the men. "My associates went to Sanborn's apartment to pick up a payment. He'd promised us half the money. Swore that he had it on him. Then they saw you exit the apartment and get arrested. "Now, where's the money?"

Briefly, Tessa wondered where in the world Maddox and Horner had been hiding to see all that go down.

She shrugged. "I don't know anything about any money." That part was true, but how was she going to get out of this confrontation? "I work for Mr. Sanborn's life insurance company," she said, thinking of the lie Cheryl told the police. "I was there to go over some paperwork on a new rider we're offering. He was already dead when I got there. I swear."

"And who's the beneficiary on this policy?" Melinda leaned forward.

Tessa shook her head. "I don't know. I didn't have access to that part of his account. I'm kinda new."

The casino manager didn't look like she believed Tessa. She pursed her lips, thinking. Finally, Melinda pushed away from the desk and rounded it to sit down again. She shuffled papers. "So, why are you here today? Did you come to play the slots? Blackjack? I'm not sure poker would suit you."

"No." Tessa shook her head. "I saw your guys pounding on my apartment door and followed them here. I don't gamble."

She didn't add that the main reason she didn't frequent the casino was she didn't have the money for it. The idea of playing a hand of poker and winning enough to pay her rent for six months was actually pretty appealing, no matter what Melinda thought of her abilities. "Now that we've had a chance to talk," she said, drawing up her courage. "And you know I don't have any information about the money Mr. Sanborn owed you, I look forward to never seeing your men at my door again."

Melinda didn't even look up. "I won't guarantee that."

Maddox moved forward and took Tessa by the elbow, giving it a pull. She yanked it out of his grasp and glared at him. He jerked his chin toward the door, making it clear the boss was finished with her and it was time to go.

Keeping her spine as straight as possible and holding her head high, Tessa left the office. She was seething inside. Melinda's holier than thou attitude had gotten to her. Just because she had like a bazillion dollars didn't mean she could treat Tessa like trash.

The two men marched Tessa back to the main floor and left her there without a word. She glowered at their retreating backs before heading toward the door.

Once again, she tried holding her breath to avoid the smoke, but it didn't work for long. She lamented her inability to go more than ten seconds without taking a breath. She really should have focused more on singing or swimming or something. You never knew when you may need to refrain from breathing for a minute or two.

As Tessa passed the blackjack table, she glanced over again, hoping the annoying guy from the restaurant, Ricardo, would be gone.

But he was still there. And now he had a visitor. Hovering just over the creepy guy's shoulder as he slammed a card on the table and shouted, "Twenty-one," was the ghost of Chet Sanborn.

Tessa stopped in her tracks, staring at the spirit. He looked much the same as the last time she'd seen him—dressed in gray polyester shorts and an ill-fitting green tank top. She could even see the ratty flip-flops on his feet. They appeared to defy gravity to stay on his feet as he hovered in the air, partly transparent.

After hesitating for a second, Tessa decided the best way to handle the situation would be to take the bull by the horns and confront the spirit head-on. As she strode toward him, wishing she'd learned how to do that force-hold thing Gloria had done on her mark, Sanborn saw her. He shook his head and then darted away.

Tessa jogged around the blackjack table, drawing the attention of the dealer, who said, "Hey, what's your hurry?"

She ignored him and kept going, but only for a few steps. Then, Sanborn disappeared through the wall. There was no way she could follow him through. Or, if there was, she didn't know how.

Biting back a curse, she smashed a fist into the other palm.

She must be the worst grim reaper in the world. That was twice she'd let a soul get away from her. She wasn't going to let it happen again.

Chapter 8

She thought about calling a cab, but Tessa decided a walk would do her some good. She could use the head-clearing time and exercise. And maybe she'd run into Sanborn's spirit again. She was determined to nab him.

The casino was on reservation land just outside the downtown area of Mist River. Tessa hurried along the shoulder of the busy interstate leading to the city a few miles away. She felt glad when she made it the half-mile into town, where the roads were far less busy and there were sidewalks.

She turned onto Whimsy Street, craving coffee or perhaps the jolt of caffeine and sugar in her favorite drink.

It was a typical small town downtown street, with a row of colorful buildings, each different, lining both sides of the block. She made a beeline for the pink one with purple shutters—Mocha and Mingle. Tessa ordered a Cuban-style cappuccino and enjoyed the scent of strong coffee with hints of chocolate and caramel while she waited to be served.

She spent a pleasant hour window shopping and sipping from her small cup before arriving back at her apartment building. With a bucket of sudsy water and a squeegee with a long handle, Silas was scrubbing windows in the lobby. He glanced at her. "Oh, good. You made it back. You know I would've picked you up if you'd called."

She nodded. She knew. But she also knew she didn't want to owe Silas many favors. She'd already paid him the rent. But with the way things were going with Chet Sanborn's spirit, there was no guarantee of next month.

"Did you find out what those guys were up to?" Silas asked.

Tessa took a sip of coffee to buy time. She wasn't sure how much to tell him. But she didn't really feel like lying either. "They thought I knew something about Mr. Sanborn's death. I let them know I didn't." She hoped he'd accept that and move on. She didn't want to tell him about Melinda or Sanborn owing the casino money.

Silas turned back toward the window.

"It's sad—Chet dying. I mean, he and I weren't friends or anything. But he paid his rent on time and didn't cause any trouble around here." He glanced over his shoulder and gave Tessa a meaningful look. "Those are nice qualities."

She rolled her eyes. "I don't cause any trouble. And I do pay my rent on time. *Mostly*. At least I don't have loud visitors over in the middle of the night."

"Yeah, yeah. Don't worry. You're not even on my short list of the most annoying tenants ever."

Her ears perked up at that and she moved closer to him to speak quietly. "Who *is* on that list?"

He clucked his tongue. "Nope. Not gonna tell you that." He held the squeegee over the bucket and wrung it out with a metal handle. "But I *will* tell you that I'm not looking forward to finding a new renter for Chet's apartment."

"Why's that?"

"Checking people's references. Interviewing them. Trying to figure out who's a good risk and who isn't—let's just say that's not my favorite part of this job."

"Sounds pretty easy to me." A wince spasmed her face—she probably shouldn't have said that.

"I guess it is easier than waitressing—or whatever it is you do now. And I have a week or so before I have to really think about it. Chet's son is up there now, cleaning his dad's stuff out."

Tessa's eyes widened. "Already? I'm surprised the cops are letting anyone in there yet."

"Yeah, the forensics team left a couple hours ago and released the apartment. Mark—that's his son's name—was already here waiting. Seemed pretty eager to get into his dad's place. "I wonder if he has siblings he wants to beat to the punch. Although, I've been in that apartment. I'm not sure his dad has anything of value. Probably just sentimental stuff." Silas stretched onto his tiptoes to get the top of the window.

Tessa was momentarily distracted by the movements of Silas' arm and back muscles. She had to pull her gaze away. There was enough going on in her life at the moment without giving in to a crush.

"Thanks again for driving me to the casino. I'll see you later."

Tessa hurried away, deciding distance was the best solution for her less than pure thoughts.

But instead of heading to her own apartment, she climbed the steps to the second floor and made her way to Sanborn's door, thinking maybe his spirit had wanted to see his son one more time before moving on. If so, Tessa could let him say his goodbyes and then help him across the veil. And if helping didn't work, she'd force him over.

That'd be nice—to be finished listening to Cheryl's lectures. At least on this particular subject.

Sanborn's door was cracked, so Tessa peeked inside. There was a young man on his hands and knees in the living room. He pawed through the drawers of a coffee table. After finding a bunch of papers, he tossed them aside, adding to a mess already piled on the floor. If Tessa didn't know any better, she'd have thought Maddox and Horner had gotten there first.

Tessa's eyes narrowed. Mark Sanborn didn't appear to be cleaning out his dad's apartment. If anything, it was the opposite. If she had to make a determination of what he was doing based on his current body language, she'd say that he was searching for something.

She cleared her throat to get his attention before pushing the door open wide and peeking in.

"Hi, there," she said in her most chipper tone. "I'm Tessa Randolph. I work for Mr. Sanborn's life insurance company. You must be his son."

Mark glanced over his shoulder, looked her up and down, and then returned to the job at hand, pulling out piles of paper and tossing them aside.

Tessa got enough of a look to see the resemblance to Chet Sanborn. He still had all of his hair, though, and he didn't wear a horrible tank top but a plain gray T-shirt and jeans.

"I'm surprised the old man had any life insurance," he mumbled. "Let me guess—I'm *not* the beneficiary."

"I don't know. I'm not actually on that part of the case. But you do have my condolences for the loss of your father. Were the two of you close?"

Mark snorted and sat back on his heels. "If by *close*, you mean *not at all interested in each other*, then yeah, we were close." He got up and moved to the entertainment center that held a small flat screen on a stand. He opened one of its cupboards and rifled through it.

"I see. I'm sorry to hear that. So, when was the last time the two of you talked?"

"We talked all the time," Mark spat. "He'd call, say he needed money, and I'd tell him to get lost. Rinse and repeat. Every week, like clockwork. Sometimes, he'd ask about his grandkids, but usually by that point in the conversation, I was pretty much done. Done talking. Done with him."

Mark closed that cupboard and moved to the one on the opposite side of the piece of furniture.

"So, your dad had some hard times, then?"

Tessa couldn't figure out what Mark was looking for. He hadn't put anything in a pile or otherwise held onto it as though it was something he planned to keep. He just kept moving from place to place in the living room.

"He didn't have hard times. He *made* hard times. Dad did fine for himself. He made a good living as a painter when he was in his thirties and forties. He could've retired once he hit sixty-five. But he couldn't stop gambling."

"I see."

"No. You don't." Mark was angry. "He was always losing. Then, when he won from time to time, things would get better. He'd take me and the family out. He'd pretend like he was going to change. But it never lasted. He might as well have been on drugs or something for as much good as his addiction did him." Mark turned toward Tessa. "We had a good relationship when I was a kid—before he found gambling. I tried to help him for a while, but he just couldn't be trusted."

Tessa's shoulders sagged. She didn't know what to say.

"In fact," Mark shook his head and frowned, "I lost a ton of money trying to help him out of his hole. But he didn't care a bit about me. I had to keep him away from my family and my stuff. The truth is I lost my dad a long time before he died. I'm glad I'm not going to have to worry about him causing me and my family any more pain. Look, I'm done in here. I'm going to look through my dad's room. Is there something else you need?"

Tessa shook her head. "I'm sorry again about your loss."

"Yeah, well, save your sorries for somebody who can use them. I don't need them." He disappeared down the hall toward the bedroom.

Tessa slipped out of the apartment.

She wondered what Mark Sanborn was looking for—was it the money he'd told the casino about?

As she headed to her apartment, she felt guilty about Mark and Chet's relationship. She and Cheryl had their differences, but she couldn't imagine being glad if her mom had died.

Something about it all just didn't add up.

Chapter 9

Tessa took a sip of coffee, winced, and tossed the Styrofoam cup in the garbage can in her tiny office. Four cups was probably too much for one morning. She was definitely channeling her nervous energy into sipping away, but her heart pounded like it was trying to escape from her chest. She opted for water to avoid some kind of cardiac event.

Movement through the doorway caught her attention. Gloria passed through the lobby, heading toward her own office.

Tessa logged out of the assignment system, which was blank for the rest of her day—maybe for the rest of forever until she caught Sanborn's soul. No new jobs meant no groceries. Maybe her neighbor Abi would take pity and feed Tessa some pizza rolls or something.

Tessa pranced out of her office and through the lobby, hoping to avoid her mother's glare but wanting to chat with her new favorite coworker.

Gloria's office was actually office-sized, unlike Tessa's janitor closet space. Tessa leaned on the doorjamb and admired the décor. The other reaper had eclectic taste. There was a mixture of modern and rustic that somehow worked together. Bright, Picasso-like paintings dotted the walls, but the desk was solid oak, heavy and sturdy. Instead of a chair, Gloria bounced on an exercise ball while she woke her computer screen with the touch of the mouse.

She glanced up, and Tessa marveled at the perfectly arranged, long false eyelashes under a coat of sparkly silver eyeshadow. "Hey. Any luck finding your guy yet?" she asked.

"I found him."

"And?"

"When he saw me, he took off."

Gloria's eyes widened. "Oh, man. You, my friend, have a runner."

Tessa groaned. She crossed a luxurious beige shag area rug to sink into a neon green futon.

"Yeah, I figured that out. But why is he running from me? I mean, it isn't like he can get his life back, right? He can't avoid passing to the other side forever, can he?"

Gloria glanced away, not meeting Tessa's eyes like her answer wasn't the one Tessa was looking for.

"Shouldn't he want to get on with things? Move on to the next phase of his existence or whatever?"

"He probably will at some point," Gloria replied. "But, right now, it seems like he has something important keeping him here. Important to him, anyway."

"What should I do?"

Gloria shrugged. "You're going to have to keep trying to tag him. Where'd you see him?"

"The casino. He was hanging out by the blackjack table."

"You don't say?" Gloria grinned and sat back in her chair. "So, either he just can't get enough gambling, even after he can't really do it anymore or . . ." She tapped the desk thoughtfully and then brightened. "Or someone there owes him something." She leaned forward and tapped the keyboard a few times. "And look at that! My next assignment is due to choke at the casino's buffet in two hours."

"Seriously?"

Gloria stood and gestured for Tessa to follow. "It won't hurt me to be a little early. Let's go see what we can find out."

Tessa leaped up and trailed after Gloria. Her heart rate had slowed back to normal, and she was glad for the company of the experienced reaper.

Once they were settled into the car and heading out of town, Tessa snuck a glance at Gloria, who had donned a pair of designer sunglasses that were huge, round, and gorgeous.

"I love your makeup," she ventured. "Where do you get it?"

Gloria shot her an amused look. "From the pharmacy." She laughed.

"Do you really?"

"I buy the cheapest stuff available and use online tutorials to make it look good."

"Wow! That's amazing."

"Oh, it's no big deal."

"I can never get mine to look anywhere near as good as yours."

"Not with that attitude! I'll help teach you if you're interested. We can have a makeup tutorial night. With wine. Obviously."

"Obviously." Tessa beamed. "That sounds great!"

Tessa very much doubted even Gloria could teach her the technicalities of applying makeup or that it would look as good on her. And she knew she wasn't the type to apply it every day. But hanging out with Gloria sounded like a lot of fun, and if she had to put up with some makeup woes to do it, then so be it.

When they got to the casino, Gloria reapplied her tangerine-colored lipstick before they went in.

The cigarette smoke hit Tessa just as hard as the last time, but it didn't take as long for her to adjust to it. The reapers wandered among the slot machines, Gloria drawing people's attention in a way Tessa never could.

When they passed the first room containing table games, Tessa spotted Ricardo there playing blackjack again. She nudged Gloria, who shrugged and followed Tessa's lead. The women flanked the man, who wore a green version of the casino tank top and held a cigar in one hand. His bushy eyebrows danced, almost touching the fringe of his toupee as he tried to look at them both at once.

"Well, hello, there." He puffed out his chest and looked smug, as though beautiful women flocked to him daily. "How you ladies doing?"

He looked closer at Tessa. "Hey, don't I know you? Yeah, I do. From that restaurant downtown, right?"

"Not anymore." Tessa sighed. "Hey, my friend and I noticed you seem to do pretty well at this." She nodded toward the cards on the table. "Can you teach us?"

"Oh, yeah. Yeah, sure." He seemed surprised but shook it off fast. "You came to the right place—the right man. I'll tell you, the dealers here hate to see me coming." He said the last part in a hushed tone, eyes darting toward the dealer, who smirked but didn't correct him.

"Great." Gloria smiled and settled into a seat. "Teach away."

Ricardo launched into a detailed but convoluted explanation of the game of blackjack. Tessa didn't pay a bit of attention. She knew the gist was to make twenty-one. Instead, she tried to appear interested while keeping an eye out for Sanborn's spirit.

"Who wants to try a hand?" Ricardo beamed at his pupils.

"I'll do it." Gloria leaned forward and put a chip on her marker before the dealer tossed out some cards.

As the other reaper played, Tessa leaned toward Ricardo and pointed at his shirt. "One of my neighbors used to wear these all the time. I didn't realize they were from the casino."

"Who was your neighbor?"

"Chet Sanborn."

Alarm flitted across his face. If Tessa hadn't been watching closely, she might've missed it. He quickly rearranged his expression into sadness.

"Oh, yeah, I knew him. It's a bummer about what happened." He seemed to be avoiding eye contact. "Do you . . . happen to know the cause of his death? The report I read didn't say. Heart attack maybe?"

Tessa shook her head. "Unfortunately, he didn't die of natural causes."

"What does that mean? He have an accident or something?"

"Someone killed him."

Ricardo nodded and tsked. "Ah. Can't say as that I'm too surprised, really. If you're going to make a living gambling, you have to hedge your bets. Get really good at one, maybe two things and stick with 'em."

"Like blackjack!" Gloria screamed as her cards made twenty-one.

Ricardo cheered and fist-pumped. "Way to go! Ha! I'm quite the teacher, eh? But honestly, any putz can make twenty-one. The real trick is to know when to split and double down."

Tessa steered the conversation back to Sanborn. "So, you were saying Mr. Sanborn didn't focus."

"Right. Chet tried to get a little bit into a lot of things instead of a lot into a few. He never got good at anything and lost a lot." He shook his head. "Kind of a shame."

Gloria tapped the table with a well-manicured nail and said, "Hit me."

"Good, good!" Ricardo praised the reaper.

"So, you think Mr. Sanborn was killed because of something to do with his gambling?" Tessa pressed, not wanting to lose the conversation thread again.

Ricardo shrugged. "I can't really say, but it wouldn't shock me if he was."

"Did he owe people money?" Tessa knew he owed the casino, but this was her chance to find out about anyone else.

He took a long pull from his cigar. "Everybody under the sun." He gave Tessa a serious look and lowered his voice. "You can't be doing that, you know? Borrowing money from folks and not paying it back. Leaves a bad taste in people's mouths. We're all just trying to get by, you know?"

Both she and Gloria nodded in agreement.

"None of us can afford to bleed out money, especially to support somebody else's habit."

"Did Sanborn owe *you* money?"

"You gotta double down on those." Ricardo disregarded Tessa in favor of Gloria's instruction.

The dealer added a three to her eight. Gloria hit again to make twenty.

Slowly, she turned toward him, expression serene. Her tone was cool but held a note of irritation. "My grandfather taught me to play blackjack when I couldn't even see over this table. And I can tell you this—you could be doing a lot better than you are."

The dealer made seventeen and shoved a stack of chips beside Gloria's. She pushed away from the table and stood.

"Too bad for you, I have to go to work and don't have time to teach you any of Granddad's tips." She winked and pushed her winnings toward Tessa. "You can have this."

Gloria started to leave and then stopped, glancing over her shoulder. "By the way. If I were you, I'd give up that horrible smoking habit. Your heart is getting tired of it."

Tessa wanted to ask Ricardo more about his relationship with Sanborn—maybe try to weasel out some information about how much money Chet had owed the other gambler. Ricardo seemed to have an attitude about Sanborn. Maybe even a motive.

But her phone buzzed, and she took it out of her purse to read the text. It was from her mother: Come over for dinner. This roast is too big for just me.

Tessa sighed. She wasn't about to turn down free food. But an evening with her mother wasn't the highest thing on her to-do list. Especially since she hadn't caught Sanborn's soul yet. She was pretty sure dinner would consist mainly of getting an earful from Cheryl.

As if she hadn't been good enough at parental lecturing, now she was also Tessa's boss. Who knew if their relationship could survive the double dose of authoritarianism.

She put away the phone and turned back toward Ricardo, but his attention was completely on the cards in his hand. The moment was gone.

Tessa left the room, scrounging up the chips that Gloria had gifted her. Maybe she could buy some cat food. She made her way toward the dining room to find Gloria. She didn't feel like walking back to town and decided she'd rather wait for the other reaper to finish up with her choker.

As she skirted around slot machines, Tessa thought about what Ricardo had said. It jived with what Officer Stewart had let slip—that Chet Sanborn had a lot of enemies who may have wanted him dead. So far, Tessa knew Melinda Chino was one of them. And Ricardo himself seemed to have motive too. Maybe Mark Sanborn could even make the cut.

How was she ever going to narrow down the list enough to figure out who the real culprit was? Because, even though Gloria had said things weren't quite as dire as Cheryl made them out to be, Tessa knew she only had so much time before a horrible tear ruptured in the veil between worlds. Or, at the very least, before she lost her job.

Chapter 10

Even though Tessa's mother wasn't exactly the cookie baking, emotionally nurturing type, going to her childhood home for one of her favorite meals was comforting. Tessa parked Linda on the curb in front of the white colonial with black shutters and gazed at it for a moment.

As always, memories and feelings came at her too fast to process. Happiness, warmth, safety, and anger rushed at her like an oncoming train. Mixed in there, overlying all of it for the past half a decade, was the pang of sadness that her father wouldn't be opening the door as she walked up the steps to the porch. He always timed it like that.

Tessa sighed and rang the doorbell, catching her breath when the front door opened. But, of course, it wasn't Michael Randolph standing there, backlit by light from the living room, smiling and then running a hand through thick, dark hair. It was Cheryl. She leaned on the door frame and waited, moving aside to let her daughter enter.

"I thought you had a key."

"Hello to you too, Mom." Tessa dropped her purse on the bench in the foyer and breathed deeply. "Dinner smells great."

"It's ready," Cheryl said. "I just need to carry the platter to the dining room."

Tessa followed through the formal foyer with its brass-framed artwork and mirrors into the big modern kitchen that glittered with stainless steel and polished black and white tile. A platter of roast and vegetables sat on the black granite countertop, and Cheryl grabbed it before heading through another doorway into the formal dining room.

"You changed the locks," Tessa said in answer to her mother's earlier question.

"That was years ago."

Tessa knew it was years ago. But she didn't visit often enough to warrant a key. Not since her dad passed.

Even though she knew what the answer would be, Tessa asked, "Can't we just eat at the kitchen table?"

She cast a wistful glance at the wood table tucked into a kitchen alcove next to a huge bay window that looked out onto the front yard's lovely landscaping. It was a homey, comforting spot that Cheryl never used for family meals.

Sure enough, Tessa's mother shook her head. "The dining room's the proper place for dinner."

She headed into the room in question, which had always made Tessa feel uncomfortable because of its formality. It reminded her of times long past. Nights when she had a boy over and her father grilled him about sports and hobbies—about school if the boy showed any hint of not being good enough for daddy's little girl.

They never were good enough.

The room was large, with oak wood floors and cream-colored walls. Paintings of food hung at intervals, and a long mahogany table, scrubbed with wood polish until you could see your reflection, stood in the center under a fancy chandelier that dripped with crystals.

Cheryl set down the platter and waited for Tessa to get to her spot. They sat simultaneously. Tessa couldn't contain a sigh as she looked at the place setting. The china was off-white with a delicate pink and blue flower pattern, and Tessa hated it. She preferred the blue everyday plates in the cupboard. Their chips and stains made her feel comfortable.

How can home not feel like home?

She reached for the red wine already poured at her place and took an unladylike gulp that drew a frown from Cheryl. "Sorry. Thanks for inviting me."

"Well, you're my daughter. And, really, this is way too much food for just one person. You can take some leftovers home too."

That sounded great to Tessa. Cheryl may not look like a fifties housewife, but she was a fantastic cook. The roast would be melt in your mouth good, that went without saying.

For a few minutes, the only sounds in the echoey dining room were utensils against plates as they served themselves and started eating. Tessa wasn't disappointed. The food was amazing. So much better than the Hot Pockets and ramen she'd gotten used to after losing her waitress job.

Then she remembered something. "Wasn't this Dad's favorite?"

Cheryl kept her eyes on her plate and nodded. "Yes. This and spaghetti."

Tessa chuckled. "Do you remember that time you asked him to make the noodles while you took a shower and he threw some against the wall to see if they were done?"

"How could I forget? He threw a whole blob along with about a half-cup of boiling water." Cheryl grinned, finally looking up. "He ruined the wallpaper."

"I helped him tear it off and repaint." Tessa laughed at the memory.

"Plus, the noodles were overdone and gooey, so we had to go out for dinner," Cheryl finished, adding her own belly laugh to Tessa's.

The room seemed to lose some of its formal stiffness as they remembered Tessa's dad's antics.

"He was always such a goofball." Cheryl shook her head and picked up her fork, poking at a carrot.

"Yeah. Dad was like the comedic relief around here." Whenever you and I got too serious or dramatic, he was always good for a dad joke or some good old slapstick."

"Us? Get dramatic? Well, I never." Cheryl grinned. "He used to say I had a flair for it. But he married me anyway."

The view of her mother blurred as a mist of tears jumped into Tessa's eyes. "I miss him."

Cheryl's face crumpled into a smile. "Me too."

Tessa tipped her head. "I've been wondering about something lately. Did Dad know what you do? I mean, what you *really* do? Or did he think you were just a life insurance agent?"

"He knew." Cheryl's words were soft, but the huge empty room made them perfectly audible.

Tessa turned that over in her mind a bit. Cheryl had held the same job for as long as she could remember. When she'd found out her mother was a reaper, it had taken Tessa a few days to come to grips with the idea. Before that, she hadn't even believed in an afterlife, spirits, or magic in any way.

"Hey, there's something I've been wanting to ask you. Being a reaper, why didn't you teach me anything about that kind of stuff when I was younger?"

Cheryl shrugged. "I didn't see the need. People believe what they want to, really, and it doesn't matter in the long run. A reaper will come for everyone, whether they know about such things or not." She set her fork down and grabbed the wine bottle to fill both their glasses.

"I guess." Tessa bit her lip, wondering whether to ask the next question. It had been on her mind since she learned her mother's true profession, but the time had never seemed right to ask. "Were you there? You know—for Dad. When he . . . when he died?"

Silence stretched for so long that Tessa thought her mother wasn't going to answer. She was surprised when Cheryl whispered, "I was there."

"So, you knew ahead of time it was going to happen?" Tessa tried to keep the accusation out of her words, but her stomach clenched in anger. Michael had died suddenly—the coroner said it was most likely some kind of congenital heart condition, even though he couldn't find any structural defect in the organ.

Tessa had woken up one morning with a dad and gone to sleep without one. There'd never been a satisfactory answer about why.

"A few hours, yes." Cheryl drank some wine, more of a gulp than a dignified sip. She set down the glass. "There was nothing I could do. There are rules, you know." She stared at the wine, not making eye contact with Tessa.

Though there was a lot more she was dying to say about the subject, Tessa swallowed the words. Her father was gone, and whether or not Cheryl could have intervened was a moot point.

Nothing could bring her dad back. She cleared her throat and changed the subject. "So, does our agency actually function as a real life insurance company? Like, do we cut checks to beneficiaries?"

Cheryl straightened, her normal cool expression settling over the pain that had been evident there for the past few minutes. "We do," she said. "And that reminds me—Mark Sanborn has a check coming. You can deliver it to him tomorrow. Just stop by the office and ask Catherine for it. She'll have it ready by nine."

Cheryl got up and started clearing dishes. "Remember to keep your eyes and ears open for anything that could lead you to Chet Sanborn's spirit. You're running out of time to catch him before there are horrible repercussions. Now, grab that roast, and I'll package some up for you to take home."

***

Mark Sanborn lived in a bungalow at the edge of town. Pride of ownership was evident in the way the place was cared for—the lawn looked like it had been trimmed on hands and knees with scissors. Not one weed dared poke its head through the cracks in the walk leading to the front stoop.

It was a pity the police officers were smashing the lovely impatiens lining it.

Tessa dove behind the neighbor's picket fence to hear what was going on.

To her credit, Mark's wife wasn't crying about the broken flowers. She wailed about her husband being taken away in handcuffs. "But he didn't kill my father-in-law!"

The distraught woman pulled on the sleeve of the closest cop, and Tessa recognized Officer Stewart. "What am I going to tell the kids when they get home?"

Stewart shrugged off her hand. "Not my problem, lady. Your husband's been charged with murder. He'll have to explain himself to the judge, not to me. I advise you to call your lawyer and tell your kids he went for a business trip."

The officer shrugged again and hurried after his comrades, who guided Mark toward a police cruiser.

The cops pulled away, leaving Mark's wife wiping her eyes on the stoop. Tessa straightened and approached cautiously. "Um. I'm sorry to bother you at a time like this."

The woman turned red-rimmed eyes toward her and sniffed. "Who are you?"

"I'm, uh, I'm Tessa Randolph. I'm from Chet Sanborn's life insurance agency. Are you Mary Sanborn?" When the woman nodded shakily, Tessa held out the check. "Your husband was Chet Sanborn's beneficiary."

Mary took the check, glanced at it, and widened her eyes before looking back at Tessa. "It's not much, but it's still a shock that he paid for life insurance at all."

Tessa nodded. Her picture of Chet Sanborn was already painted. At this point, she wasn't in need of more details unless they led to catching his spirit.

"At least this will cover the costs for his wake tonight." Mary winced and glanced the direction the police cars had gone. "Mark is going to miss it, I guess."

"That's terrible," Tessa said. "Maybe he'll get processed quickly and released in time . . . when is it? Is it close by?" She tried to couch the prying in an empathetic tone, already planning ways to crash the wake. Perhaps Chet Sanborn's spirit would be there. Gloria had said some of them run from their reaper because they want to attend their funeral.

Mary sniffed and rubbed her eyes one last time. She turned toward the house. "It's at six tonight in the big room you can rent at Frank's Bar and Grill." She shrugged. "Not fancy, but neither was Chet. And it's affordable." She waved the check. "Thanks for this. I need to get inside and call our lawyer."

As Tessa watched Mary disappear into the house, she fought off the groan that wanted to tear out of her throat. Of course Chet's wake had to be at the very last place Tessa wanted to go.

As she spun around to head back toward Linda, she bolstered herself with the thought that Frank probably wouldn't even be there. Her ex liked to be home by five to watch movies and eat snacks in his underwear. He usually had staff handle any parties that rented out the big room in the back of the bar in the evenings.

She felt better at that thought.

Yeah. It'll be fine. Frank won't even be there.

Chapter 11

Wearing a knee-length navy blue A-line dress covered with white flowers and one-inch beige pumps, Tessa drove to Frank's Bar and Grill. The drive still felt familiar—the muscle memory of the daily routine, driving there, sometimes twice a day for double shifts, took over. She was able to let her mind wander while her brain automatically handled Linda, whose stubborn phase seemed to be over—at least for a little while.

She stared out at the sun setting on the horizon, thinking about Chet Sanborn and how tragic his life had ended. Had he really been killed by his own son? But that line of thought, paired with the fact that she was going to a wake, quickly led to other thoughts. She couldn't help but think about her dad.

Michael Randolph had been a kind man—the kindest. Tessa remembered him giving his services as a lawyer pro bono for those who found themselves in need of a defense attorney but without the means to get a good one. And he was a good one. He'd spread his books and papers out over the kitchen table in the evening and pore over old cases, searching for the best way to help his clients. Sure, he had paying ones too. Usually, they were rich people from the city. Essentially, they paid for Tessa's dad to help the others.

As a result, the Randolphs never had the fancy summer house down south that most of Michael's lawyer friends had. And sometimes, Cheryl would raise an eyebrow when Michael took on *another* case for free. At times like those, Michael would grab Cheryl by the waist, swing her around the living room to imaginary music, and make her laugh. He'd make all three of them laugh.

He'd been a great dad and husband.

Tessa remembered going to his funeral but only barely. The whole thing had been a blur. People gave her their condolences. There were lots of hugs. And everyone had a story about her father. Many of them were the people he had helped. Those he'd stood up for in a system that seemed designed to beat them.

Pulling into the parking lot at the bar, Tessa shook off those memories. She needed to stay sharp and have her full concentration on the task at hand. If Chet Sanborn's spirit showed up, she needed to reel him in. She had to get him to the other side so they could both move on—and she could collect her paycheck.

It felt strange going in the front door of the establishment after years through the back door. But instead of nostalgia, a wave of relief wafted over her. She'd always hated walking past that stinky dumpster and feeling the wave of dry kitchen heat smack her in the face. Going through the front was much nicer. More human.

Frank's Bar and Grill was the quintessential neighborhood spot. Its log construction and hand-carved wooden bar were both rugged and quaint. Frank had inherited the place from his father, which made it easier for him to turn a profit—he didn't have a mortgage, so the overhead was limited to payroll, maintenance, and supplies.

Still, Frank was a decent businessman. The place was always bustling. There were pool tables and dart boards. Big flatscreen TVs lined the walls beside the bar. And he served both domestic and craft brews on draught, so the place drew in crowds of all variety.

Tessa stopped in the doorway to look around and get her bearings. A large folding sign in the small lobby proclaimed the place to be closed for a special event. At the bottom, it said RIP Chet Sanborn. She peeked through the doorway. Several people were bunched around the bar, but it wasn't nearly as busy as a normal Friday night. Plus, it was quieter, more subdued, than the weekend crowd would be.

Mary Sanborn stood near the back of the room, near a long table loaded with food, talking to an older couple. She held two elementary-age kids to her sides, but the children's eyes darted around as though they wanted to run off and get into some mischief.

"Well, well. Look who's here."

Tessa winced and turned to face Frank.

Crud!

She'd really thought he wouldn't be there. But there he was—all six feet and four inches of him, looking as handsome as ever. He wore black pants and a shirt that looked tailored for him, but Tessa knew he bought them off the rack at Maverick's Big & Tall on Main Street. He was lucky to be proportioned just right for non-tailored clothes, even if he did have to go to the ritzy shop.

Frank's grandparents had come over from Sicily, and he had distinctly Italian features, including thick, curly black hair and olive skin. He grinned, and her heart did a strange little dance. *Traitor!*

"Yeah," she said meekly. "I came for Mr. Sanborn's wake. He was my neighbor. Remember?"

She purposely removed her gaze from Frank's appealing physique and placed it back on the wake-goers. She cursed herself for ending with a question, as if she wanted to talk to Frank—as if she wanted him to remember anything about their relationship.

"I, uh, yeah. I remember."

Tessa didn't see Chet's spirit anywhere. If he did show, she thought he'd be hanging around near Mary or the children.

"I'm sorry for your loss." Frank didn't sound sorry. "But I'm glad to see you." He stepped closer.

Alarm bells started going off in Tessa's mind. *What's he doing?* He was within what most Americans would consider their personal space bubble. She stepped back an equivalent amount of space and narrowed her eyes at him. "Yeah. Thanks."

"You know, it's been weird around here without you." Another step forward. "Weird not having you hang out at my apartment too. I miss you."

Tessa stepped back again but jumped as her spine hit the maitre d's lectern.

Trapped.

For a second, she wavered. Maybe being pursued by a handsome man who missed her wasn't such a bad thing. Maybe Frank had learned his lesson and would treat her more like Tessa's dad had treated her mom if she took him back and less like a king treats the chamber maid.

"I miss you, baby."

That word. It snapped her wholeheartedly back to reality. Tessa shook her head to clear it out. *No way.* Frank had missed his chance. He might be feeling nostalgic and acting charming now, but she knew from experience he'd be back to his old ways in no time flat.

She considered using some of the skills she'd learned in the jujitsu class she took the previous summer to get Frank out of her space. But it was one class, and she barely remembered it. She decided to take a more civilized approach. "Aw, that's a nice thing to say, Frankie. Hey, does that mean you've got that check ready—you know, the one you owe me with all that back pay?"

Irritation flitted across his face.

Bingo. She'd been right. Frank hadn't changed, and he wasn't going to. He was the same old user he'd always been.

He stepped back. "I don't know what you're talking about. I don't owe you a red cent." He turned and nodded toward the expediting window. "It looks like Louie needs me at the kitchen. Gotta run."

As Tessa watched him hightail it to the kitchen, she sighed in relief. It felt like she'd dodged a major bad choice. There was no doubt in her mind she was better off without Frank.

After taking a minute to gather herself, Tessa stepped into the restaurant's main room. Mary and the kids were getting food at the buffet.

Another scan of the room for Chet's spirit turned up nothing. But her gaze did land on someone she knew. Ricardo Vidale. He sat on a barstool, back to the bar as he drank a beer and surveyed the room. His toupee looked the best she'd ever seen it, as though he'd washed and combed it for the wake. He spotted Tessa before she could dart into the crowd and waved her over.

Reluctantly, Tessa approached him, forcing a smile onto her face. "Hey, there. How are you?"

He lifted the beer. "Just fine now that I have this in my hand."

Tessa thought she might need something too—if this conversation wasn't quick.

He looked her up and down, creepy as always. "It's good to see you in here again, even if you aren't serving my burger."

"With an extra pickle!"

He smiled, and she thought he really shouldn't.

"It does feel kind of weird to be in here and not rushing around taking orders."

"How about I buy you a beer?" Ricardo suggested. "You know, for old time's sake. Or, how about for Chet. That jerk can't drink anymore, so we might as well have one or two for him."

Tessa opened her mouth to agree—why not have a beer she didn't have to pay for? But before she could say the word, a movement near the ceiling a few feet away caught her attention. She whipped her head around to focus on it. Sure enough, Chet Sanborn's spirit hovered there. When he saw her looking at him, he flew toward the kitchen. "I, uh, I gotta go!"

"Rain check," Ricardo called after her.

She dashed after Chet.

While he had the benefit of flying over everyone's heads—he even went right through a woman's hat—Tessa had to go around people.

When Chet's semi-transparent form disappeared into the kitchen, Tessa hesitated, then groaned. She plowed through the swinging door after him. The ghost headed straight toward the back door with Tessa barreling along behind him. She dodged one of the cooks, who swore at her.

"Wash out your mouth, Louie," she said out of habit.

She caught a glimpse of Frank's shocked face looking at her from his tiny office tucked off the corner of the big kitchen, but she didn't slow down. Tessa hit the easy-push bar handle of the back door and burst out into the alley. The irony wasn't lost on her. She'd been so happy to avoid the stinky back entrance, and there she was anyway, trying to breathe through her mouth to avoid the horrible odor. It smelled like week-old buffet, a bit sweet and a lot sour.

Dusk had fallen, and Tessa stumbled to a halt so she didn't run into something as her eyes adjusted to the dimness. She looked around wildly, heart pounding as she worried that she'd lost her mark again. But she caught a glimpse of him heading out of the short alley into the employee parking lot and raced after him, cursing the fact that she was wearing heels.

When she hit the parking lot's asphalt, Tessa considered removing the shoes and running in bare feet, but she knew that would risk cutting herself on glass or worse. Keeping a neat employee parking lot wasn't Frank's strong suit. He preferred to focus on the front of the restaurant and even that was iffy at times.

Chet's spirit slowed and spun around as though checking to see if the reaper was still after him.

"Stop!" Tessa couldn't shout as loudly as normal because she was already out of breath. "I just want to talk to you for a minute."

Chet shook his head. He looked almost solid for a second, but when he turned and the light from a nearby street lamp hit him, his form was semi-transparent again. "You want to send me to the great beyond. I can't go. Not yet."

"Why?" she crowed after him. "It's the next stage in your journey. There's nothing to be afraid of."

"I'm not afraid. I just need to tell my son I'm sorry."

Tessa took a few steps forward, but the spirit flitted backward an equal distance. "Your son? Mark?"

The ghost nodded.

"But he killed you. Didn't he? He was arrested this afternoon."

"No," Chet argued. "That isn't right. My boy would never do that."

Tessa used the moment of distraction to edge forward again. "When I talked to Mark, he seemed pretty angry with you."

Sanborn reached up and scratched a spot in the ring of hair, just like he'd done routinely when he was alive. Tessa wondered if ghosts had itches or if they just retained the habits from their living days. "I didn't say he didn't have a right to do it. I just said he didn't."

"Then who did?"

Sanborn's spirit made eye contact with Tessa. It caused a chilly feeling to run up her back. He shrugged. "I don't know. I had a lot of enemies. I owed a lot of people money and didn't play by the rules. Even the rules of criminals.

"But my boy is innocent. And I'm just not ready to go." In the blink of an eye, Sanborn dove into the street light's pole and was gone.

Tessa growled and clenched her fists. She hung around for ten minutes watching the orange glow of the light, figuring Chet would have to come out eventually. But her stomach started grumbling, and with another groan of frustration, she turned back toward the restaurant.

Maybe she could still get Ricardo to buy her that beer.

Chapter 12

The next morning, Tessa was dragging. She had a blister on each heel from the stupid pumps. And that morning, she'd stepped in cat puke—of course Pepper had the gall to look innocent.

Seriously, how hard was it to find an out-of-the-way, easy-to-clean spot to bring up a hairball? But, noooo. The cat had to leave it right beside the bed where Tessa was sure to place her first footfall of the day.

Oh, and she hadn't caught Chet Sanborn's spirit, so the world was probably going to end soon. When it did, it would be entirely her fault.

Talk about a bad week.

That's why she headed into the office on a Saturday. She couldn't sleep, and the four walls of her apartment had seemed to be closing in on her. Or maybe it was the air there, threatening to constrict her throat.

Tessa had to find Chet Sanborn's spirit before it was too late. But at least she knew why he was still here. He wanted to tell Mark that he was sorry. And he probably wanted to know who had killed him—if it wasn't Mark. Tessa realized she'd like to know that too.

Tessa needed her space to cool off and think.

The office was abandoned when she got there, so Tessa spent twenty minutes figuring out how to work the industrial-size coffee maker. In the end, she had to make a full pot, so now there was enough coffee for her to avoid sleeping for about a week.

But coffee hadn't even helped break her bad mood. She was on her second cup and sitting at her desk when even those four walls felt more confining than her apartment's. On a whim, she went into her mother's office to have a look around. Cheryl would probably call this snooping.

There wasn't much to look at. Its minimalistic décor was even more striking since Tessa was looking for something to occupy her mind.

Then her gaze fell on the filing cabinet and she had an idea. She set her coffee on the desk and opened the cabinet. Her hand trembled slightly, hovering over the files as she hesitated. Then she flipped through to the Rs. Her heart pounded wildly as she went through the alphabet, looking for Randolph.

But there was no file for Michael Randolph.

"You're looking in the wrong spot, Theresa."

Tessa whirled around to face her mother, who leaned against the door frame nonchalantly.

"I, uh, I am?"

Cheryl crossed to the desk, picked up Tessa's coffee, and handed it to her. Then, she opened a desk drawer and pulled out a canister of wipes. She used one to wipe the spot on the desk where the coffee had sat.

"I didn't expect you to come in today," Tessa said.

"Well, I can see that," her mother said. "I assume you wouldn't rifle through my things if you expected me to show up at any moment. And I assume you're looking for your father's file."

Tessa shrugged and looked at her feet. "What makes you think that?"

"Because there isn't anyone else's file you'd be interested in." Cheryl paused and drummed her fingers on the glass desk. "His paperwork isn't filed under his name."

"Why . . . why not?"

Cheryl paused and pursed her lips. It alarmed Tessa because her mother didn't usually have to stop and think about what to say. Words came easily to her, and she didn't put her foot in her mouth like her daughter did routinely.

Finally, Cheryl let out a long breath. "Because he wasn't supposed to die that day."

She'd spoken so softly that Tessa wasn't sure she'd heard right. Her voice cracked when she asked, "Did you say Dad wasn't supposed to die?"

Cheryl didn't look up. She only nodded.

Tessa sank into the opposite chair. "What does that even mean? How does that . . ." She thought for a minute. "Was he murdered or something?"

But even as the words slipped out, she knew that wasn't right. Chet Sanborn had been murdered—and reaping his spirit had shown up as an assignment for Tessa. So, even murders were *expected* as far as the universe was concerned.

Her mother verified her thought process with a shake of her head. With her lips pressed tightly together, she finally made eye contact with her daughter. She leaned forward. "Your dad took someone else's place."

"Whose?" Tessa felt a sinking feeling like a weight had been flung inside her belly.

Cheryl paused, wincing as though the words were causing her physical pain. "Theresa, *you* were slated to die that day."

Over the years, Tessa had heard the phrase about feeling like the air was being sucked out of the room, but before then, it had just been a saying. A cliché without real meaning. Until that moment.

Tessa felt as though she couldn't get enough air into her lungs. They burned like she'd run a marathon. She gasped and choked. This was worse than her apartment ever dared to be.

Cheryl looked sympathetic. Beside the wipes in her drawer, she found a box of tissues. She took one for herself and passed Tessa the box.

"I saw it on another reaper's schedule by accident. You were supposed to get electrocuted by our stupid, old toaster—if you can believe it. I was totally distraught. I told your father, and he was calm. He grabbed my hands and said it was all going to be okay. Then he went into the kitchen and grabbed the toaster. He took it into the garage and beat it with a hammer. He asked me to distract you, so I made some pancakes and took them up to your room."

Tessa remembered those pancakes like they were the last vestiges of happiness in her life.

"Then, your dad told me to stay out of the kitchen," Cheryl continued. "He didn't want me to get in trouble at work for what he was about to do. But I peeked around the door frame without them knowing. I saw it all. When Sylvia, the reaper who was supposed to take you, arrived in our home, your dad opened his arms wide and begged her to take him instead. At first, she refused. But eventually, she agreed."

"Why?"

Cheryl looked so sad as a small smile tilted up her lips. "She was a mom too."

"So, he exchanged himself for me?" Tessa said, amazed she'd found the air to speak. "That's allowed?"

Cheryl shook her head, and her tone was sharp. "No. It isn't allowed. Sylvia almost lost her job, and there was a big to-do over it. You don't even want to know all the red tape it created. It's still not completely settled." She reached across the desk and squeezed Tessa's hands. "But you're here. It's what your dad wanted."

So many thoughts swirled through Tessa's mind that she couldn't seem to catch one. Her dad wasn't supposed to die. She was. She shouldn't be there right now, talking to her mom and feeling the throb of blisters on her heels. She should be on the other side doing . . . whatever spirits did there. *Float around and wax philosophical, maybe? Watch their loved ones struggle on earth and send healing energy?*

She had no idea how to feel about what she'd just learned. She just felt lost. A new form of grief washed over her. Guilt.

"That paperwork you were looking for is still under your name," Cheryl said. "If you'd looked a bit beyond the Ms to the Ts, you would have found it. But it's not really something you need to read."

"Why didn't you tell me?"

Cheryl shook her head. "Michael asked me not to. And I didn't see any point in adding that pain to your plate. Losing your dad was hard enough."

She was right about that. Tessa wanted to take the box of tissues and cry in bed all day.

But Cheryl stood up and spoke more firmly. "And I don't want you to start feeling guilty or anything like that. Parents make sacrifices for their kids. Your dad was happy to make the one that he did. He loved you. I love you."

Tessa didn't answer. It was too late. Guilt had already crept its way into her from every angle, like primordial black, tarry ooze, invading her peace. She shouldn't be alive. Her dad had missed out on over half his life. And for what? So his daughter could be a waitress with no prospects—living paycheck to paycheck in a crappy apartment?

"Reaper work is complicated, Theresa," Cheryl said, studying her daughter's face. "There are a lot of nuances to it. You're already learning that lesson well with Chet Sanborn. Sometimes, things don't go the way they're supposed to. All facets of life are complicated. Even death. It's best not to overthink all the whys and wherefores. Just keep on doing your job. And right now, for you, that means finding your mark before he sets off a fracture between the worlds."

Chapter 13

Tessa stood outside of work trying to get her lungs to work properly again. The news about her dad had left her shocked and exhausted. She wasn't sure what to do next. It was as though her day—her life—had gone completely sideways.

She allowed herself to wallow for a few minutes while the sun beat on her face. It had already chased away some of the spring morning chill, and sunlight glared off Linda's windshield.

Tessa straightened her shoulders and marched toward the car. The thing about her dad was going to take a while to process. She was pretty sure sleep was going to be a thing of the past for a long time coming. But there were other things to do in the meantime. Like find Chet Sanborn's spirit.

She was still confused about whether not finding him would cause some kind of demon apocalypse or if Gloria was right and it was no big deal. She didn't really want to find out, and beyond that, she wanted to finish the job she'd set out to do.

After that . . . well, she wasn't sure. Something had begun to niggle at her mind. Anger. She was angry with the reaper who took her dad instead of her. Angry at all reapers in general.

She didn't think she wanted to be one after this. But that was a decision for another day.

Linda must have caught on to Tessa's black mood because she didn't cause any trouble, starting right away. In fact, she sounded like someone had given her a whole new engine. Tessa nodded in satisfaction. "That's what I'm talkin' about." She patted the dashboard. "Good girl."

For a minute, she bit her lower lip and wondered where to go next. She glanced at the clock. It was lunchtime.

She headed to Frank's Bar and Grill. She wasn't sure why—except that it was the last place she'd seen Chet Sanborn's spirit. She knew he wasn't likely to be there again—not since the wake was over. But it was as good a place as any to start her search anew.

Plus, after Ricardo had talked them up, she had a craving for one of Frank's cheeseburgers.

Speak of the devil.

Ricardo sat at the bar again, hunched over his meal. Tessa was surprised—she'd figured the creepy guy would spend most of his time at the casino. The night before, she downed her beer fast, paid her respects to Mary Sanborn, and left.

Maybe she should spend a bit more time talking to Ricardo this time. He seemed like he hadn't been telling her the full story.

She sat next to him, earning herself a big, missing-tooth smile. She forced herself to smile back. "Oh, hey. Fancy meeting you here again."

"Right back at ya, girlie. You've been here more lately than when you worked here." He guffawed at his own joke, sloshing a little beer out of his glass. He wiped his hand on his pants. "Oh, hey, you want another beer?"

Or course she didn't. It was barely noon. Still, she'd had a rough morning, so she did give it some thought.

"No. I think I'm going to have a burger. Then I need to get going."

She ordered from the bartender and then sipped the ice water he'd dropped off.

"Ya know," Ricardo began, "I was surprised to see you at Chet's wake last night. I never saw you hanging out with him or anything before he died."

"He was my neighbor." She shrugged. "Hanging out isn't the right term for our relationship. But I felt compelled to pay my respects."

"Compelled, huh." Ricardo took a gulp of his beer. "That's one way to think about it."

Tessa paused and then decided to see if she could get some information flowing. "Yeah, well, it's true. I've learned some interesting things about Chet these past few days."

"Interesting how?" Ricardo took the bait.

"Melinda Chino told me Chet owed the casino money. Do you know anything about that?"

Ricardo's bushy eyebrows traveled upward. "Nah," he scoffed. "That's gotta be a lie. If anything, it's the other way around. Chet won the grand prize at the blackjack tournament just a couple weeks ago. I don't know if he managed to get paid before he checked out."

Ricardo grabbed a handful of nuts from a bowl in front of him and munched away.

Tessa leaned back to get out of range of any peanut dust that may fly out of the unpleasant man's mouth. But what he'd said was interesting. Could Melinda have owed Sanborn money? If that was the case, why had she sent her goons to his apartment? And then to *her* apartment? Could she have been trying to get the prize money back?

Her brow furrowed as she thought about it. None of it made any sense. Why would the casino put on a tournament and then try to steal the prize money back after it was awarded?

Tessa could only think of one reason. She continued to lean back since Ricardo was still eating nuts. "Do you know if the casino is having financial problems or something?"

The waiter dropped off Tessa's burger while Ricardo looked longingly at his empty pint glass but didn't order another one. He sighed and shoved the peanut bowl aside. "Not that I know of. I mean, it's a casino. People are there spending money all day every day. How could they be low on money?"

Tessa nodded. He made a good point.

"I mean," he continued, "Melinda Chino seems to be making a mint. She's building a new house on fifty acres outside of town. The place looks like a mansion. You should see it—it's only framed in right now, but it's got two towers. One on each side. Regular Rapunzel towers. You know the type." He chuckled and shook his head. "She must have more money than you or I would see in ten lifetimes."

Lifetimes. Tessa pondered the word. She couldn't help thinking about her dad and the half a lifetime he'd wasted on her. She knew that, from then on out, she'd have to stop squandering it.

Ricardo climbed unsteadily off the barstool. "I'll be right back."

She chewed and watched him retreat toward the men's room, mulling over what he'd said. Melinda was building a big, fancy house off her casino earnings. Was that normal for a manager? Tessa supposed the woman could be independently wealthy.

But maybe there was a different explanation. Maybe she was siphoning money from the casino. Could she have killed Sanborn to steal back the blackjack money for herself?

Deciding she needed to make a point to talk to Melinda again, Tessa left some cash on the bar for the burger and hurried out of the restaurant before Ricardo could get back from the men's room.

It bothered her a tiny bit that she didn't even feel bad about it.

Chapter 14

The next day was warmer, and Tessa wore denim shorts and a red cap sleeve shirt to the office. She figured her mother would get after her about her wardrobe or, at the very least, raise a perfect eyebrow. But Tessa didn't care. She was fed up.

She'd spent the night sitting on the sofa, stroking a purring Pepper and thinking about reapers. The more she sat and thought, the angrier she got. What kind of job expected people to escort souls to the other side? It must be the absolute worst job in existence.

As dawn got closer and Tessa dove deeper into her emotions, she began to realize she was angry at someone she really didn't want to ever be mad at. Her father. She'd buried her face in Pepper's soft fur and groaned. "Why did you do it, Dad? You still had a long life ahead of you. It was supposed to be me."

The cat looked at her with confusion plastered on her sleepy kitty face.

Tessa couldn't help but laugh. "Not you, fur ball. You're okay."

Her phone had dinged, making both of them jump. It was an assignment.

Tessa narrowed her eyes as she studied the screen. She didn't want to be a reaper anymore. She'd made the decision. Someone else would have to take the assignment—maybe Gloria needed the extra money.

Her phone had chimed again. This time it was a text from her mother.

"I know it's hard right now. But I gave you another assignment. You should get the notification any minute if you haven't already."

Tessa rolled her eyes. Her mother acted as if she was doing her a favor. Cheryl could do it herself. Tessa was out.

And if no one found Chet Sanborn's spirit and the world ended in a war between spirits and live people, Tessa would lock herself in the apartment with Pepper and live on noodles and peanut butter until it was over. So, basically, nothing would change.

She made sure to show up at the office with plenty of time before the assignment. That way, Cheryl would have one less thing to judge her about—aside from her attire. There was plenty of time for another reaper to get there in time.

Tessa crossed the marble floor, heading straight for her mother's office. The blisters on her heels felt better, but she'd still put on Band-Aids inside her blue Chuck Taylors.

Cheryl's office was empty. So was Gloria's. In fact, the only person Tessa could find in the entire building was the janitor, who was finishing up and heading out.

"It's Sunday," he told her. "Y'all usually work from home on Sunday."

Pursing her lips, Tessa thought about jotting down a quick resignation letter and leaving it on her mother's desk. But she glanced at the clock above the reception desk.

"Ugh," she groaned. "There's no way someone else can get there in time."

The assignment was at a nursing home on the other side of town. If she couldn't make contact with another reaper right then, no one would be there when Ellen Walker passed.

Then there could be two souls wandering around Mist River.

With a groan, Tessa stomped out the door, resigned to the fact that she'd need to do one last assignment before she could retire her reaper powers.

Fine. One more.

At least then, she could pay a couple more bills or maybe get groceries. She was running out of peanut butter. And who knew how long it would be before she could find another job, get hired, and work long enough for another paycheck.

Yeah. Maybe this is a good thing.

Tessa tried not to wonder too much why Linda was cooperating so well lately. It felt like one of those situations when, if she gave it thought or attention, it would go sour on her. So, she just gave a silent cheer when the engine roared to life and then tried to act like it was an everyday occurrence.

When she got to the Mist River Senior Home, Tessa checked the time. On her phone, not Linda's slow clock. She had five minutes to figure out where Ellen's room was and get there. Should be plenty of time, in theory.

The nursing home was old but sparkling clean and cheerfully decorated. It looked more like someone's home than a hotel, which Tessa found soothing. The lobby was filled with plants and bright paintings, and a small desk stood in the corner instead of a big doctor's office-style window.

No one sat behind the desk.

Tessa hurried over and rang the bell. She waited, tapping her foot, for a minute, but time was getting away from her. Thinking about how she'd been too late to escort Mr. Sanborn over and the huge mess that ensued, she figured she'd better be proactive about finding Ellen.

Her maternal grandmother had lived in the home, so Tessa knew her way around a bit. She pictured the layout for a moment—there was one wing for men and another for women. She headed toward the women's wing, entering the long hallway through a metal door.

The cheerful décor continued in the hallway—more plants, paintings, and tables. Tessa hurried along, glancing into each open door she came to, hoping Ellen wasn't behind one of the few closed ones.

About halfway down, on the left, Tessa found her. And she was too late. Ellen had already passed away. Her spirit stood next to the still form on the bed. Well, at least she'd stayed put. She hadn't run like Sanborn did when her reaper wasn't johnny-on-the-spot.

Tessa moved into the room. It reminded her of her grandmother, all decorated in pale pink and pastel green. Lace doilies covered every available surface, and silver-framed pictures of Ellen and her family made up the main decoration.

Ellen smiled at Tessa. "Hello, dear. I'm glad you could make it."

"Sorry I'm late." Tessa smiled. "I'm new and still getting the hang of all this."

"Oh, don't you worry yourself about it." Ellen gazed lovingly at her physical form, brushing a transparent hand over her own cheek. "It was a good body, and in the end, I went in my sleep."

"So did my grandmother," Tessa said.

Ellen beamed back at her. "I couldn't have asked for a better life or death."

Tessa couldn't help but think of her dad. He hadn't gotten the good, long life that Ellen had. He didn't even have much time to contemplate the rest of his life. His reaper had let him sacrifice himself.

Ellen's spirit floated away from her body, stopping at a framed photo of her younger self, smiling next to a handsome man. "I can't wait to see Walter. Do you know, will it be very long before I can be with him?"

"I, uh, I don't know the answer to that."

Ellen waved off the apology. "Oh, that's right. You're new. It's okay. I guess I'll find out soon enough!"

"Yeah, it's probably time to go." Tessa wanted to get back to the agency and put in her resignation. She waved a hand, and a beam of light shot into the room as though someone had opened a skylight. She reached out for Ellen's spirit. "Are you ready?"

"Yes, dear. I am." Ellen turned away from her body. She shot Tessa one more smile.

Tessa reached out and touched the spirit. It didn't feel like anything, but suddenly, she felt like she was moving—rising into the beam of light. They traveled together like that for a few moments. Tessa glanced at Ellen's spirit. Her expression was serene. Hopeful. Happy.

She looked beautiful.

Suddenly, Ellen gasped and pointed. Ahead of them, a figure stood, backlit by the white light. As they got closer, Tessa could see it was an elderly man. She stopped short and let Ellen go ahead. She floated toward the other spirit, who opened his arms to embrace her tenderly.

Tears sprang to Tessa's eyes. She could feel the joy emanating from both spirits. They were at peace, finally reunited at the end of long, happy lives.

The spirits parted, and the man offered his elbow to Ellen, who accepted it readily. They floated away, blinking out of Tessa's view after a moment.

In the next instant, Tessa was back in Ellen's room. The light was gone. She slipped out and hurried back toward the lobby, filled with emotion, still wiping tears from her eyes. What she'd just witnessed—the reunion she'd facilitated with her reaper power—had been nothing short of breathtakingly beautiful. Tessa felt honored to have witnessed it.

She emerged from the nursing home into the sun and looked to the sky, imagining Ellen and her husband dancing with the stars, still in love even in the next leg of their journey. She smiled and breathed deeply, feeling her heart settle into an easier rhythm than she'd felt in days.

She shook her head, thinking about her mother. Cheryl knew exactly what she was doing. Maybe Tessa didn't want to give up her new job after all.

Chapter 15

Tessa decided to head home for some lunch and figure out her next move for finding Chet Sanborn. She realized that crossing over wasn't necessarily as scary as Chet probably thought. Or at least it didn't have to be. She just had to convince Chet. Things would resolve themselves on Earth with or without him. But she did hope that everything with his son Mark found a resolution soon.

Silas was in the lobby, taking a rare break and sitting behind the front desk doing nothing. He smiled, revealing those irresistible dimples. He nodded toward the sun streaming through the front windows. "Nice day."

"Yeah, it's wonderful out."

"If only I wasn't stuck inside."

"What? Are you out of repairs to work on?"

He snorted. "Never. I'm just taking a breather."

"That's so . . . unlike you."

"I'm taking a play out of your playbook," he said. "Oh, by the way, I saw Officer Stewart at the hardware store this morning. We had an interesting conversation."

"About?"

"Well, about grout mostly."

"And?"

"And he told me they released Mark Sanborn."

Tessa pursed her lips, thinking. "So, they can't prove he did it."

"Usually," Silas said, "they don't make an arrest until they're pretty sure they can prove it. I'm thinking he must have had an alibi that checked out and overwhelmed their proof."

"That's what you think, huh?"

Silas shrugged. "I watch a lot of *Law & Order*."

"Hmm." She leaned on the desk and studied him for a moment. She knew Chet Sanborn wanted to talk to his son. If he was at home, maybe she'd find the errant spirit there. Since she'd decided to keep her reaper job, apprehending him was back on her short list of things to get done.

"Okay, well, I'll see you later." She turned toward the door.

"Where are you going?" He sounded suspicious. "You just got here—you didn't even go to your apartment yet."

She bit her bottom lip. "Um. I just remembered an errand I need to run." She winced, hearing her own tone sounding like an evasion. Tessa had never been a good liar.

"Listen," Silas said, "If you're going to Mark Sanborn's house, I'm going with you. I learned my lesson last time."

"You did?"

"After I dropped you off at that casino, I worried about you like crazy. Felt like a horrible friend for leaving you there in a possibly dangerous situation. I don't want to deal with that again—it'll throw off my whole day." He came around the counter. "And I'll drive. I don't feel like getting stranded by that bucket of rust you call a car."

"Hey! Linda isn't rusty. She's just . . . finicky." Tessa followed him out to his Silverado. Tessa gave Linda a frown. "Don't tell her, but I'm saving up for something newer and more reliable."

"That's nice." He fired up the truck's engine. "And in the meantime, I can probably keep her going for you."

"You know how to fix cars too?" Tessa wondered what this man couldn't do.

"Some," he said. "My dad and I used to work on them a lot when I was a kid. I picked up some tricks. So, where's this guy live?"

Tessa gave him directions to Mark and Mary Sanborn's house and enjoyed the feeling of the warm cab as they drove over. They turned into the large suburban community where the houses all shared design aesthetics and the same size lots. People were outside, walking or playing catch in their yards. After the cold, rainy snap they'd had, everyone was soaking up the sun.

They pulled up in front of the Sanborns' house and got out. Tessa hurried around the truck and intercepted Silas. "You can wait here for me if you want."

He shook his head. "Nope. I'm coming in with you."

"Why?" Having a driver was one thing, but Silas would definitely interfere if she found Chet's spirit. He'd probably think she went crazy if she started talking to an unseen entity.

"I'm not convinced the cops didn't let a murderer go free." He crossed his flannel-clad arms. "And I'm not sending you in to face a killer alone. Sorry. You're stuck with me."

She eyed him for a moment. His face was set into hard lines, and his shoulder and arm muscles looked tense. He resembled a dangerous, angry lumberjack. "Fine. But let me do the talking, okay? You're kind of . . . intimidating right now."

His brow furrowed. "I'm not intimidating. I'm totally guy-next-door friendly."

That was true most of the time. Silas was the type of guy people wanted to tell their life story.

"Maybe *you* should stay here while *I* talk to Mark." Smugness oozed out of his body language.

Tessa rolled her eyes. "Let me do the talking, Mr. Guy-next-door."

"Are you going to tell me what this is all about, Tessa?" Silas asked as they opened the picket fence to the yard. "It's about your new job, isn't it?"

"Maybe."

"You're not going to be telling any lies to get answers, are you? Because, honestly, you're terrible at it."

"And you're a good liar, huh?" She climbed the steps to the stoop and then dug in her purse for a ponytail holder to pull back her long hair.

Silas shrugged. "I haven't had much occasion to lie in my life, but anyone would be better at it than you. You have a tell."

"I do?"

He nodded. "You bite your bottom lip right before you say something untrue. It's a basic, beginner's tell. You should work on it if you intend to do much lying."

She blinked at him, dumbfounded. Tessa had no idea it was that easy to see she was lying, but it explained so much. Like how her dad had *always* known when she was lying as a teenager. "Huh. I didn't know I did that."

"Yeah, well, stick with this life insurance thing, okay? I don't think we'll be seeing you on World Series of Poker anytime soon." He chuckled.

Before she could stop herself, Tessa bit her bottom lip, just thinking about the lie that she was strictly a life insurance agent. Luckily, Silas wasn't looking at her—he was knocking on the door. She forced her lip back out and straightened her spine.

Mary Sanborn answered the door. She looked confused until she glanced past Silas and spotted Tessa. "Oh, hello again. Is there some paperwork or something that got missed?"

Tessa shook her head. "No, I was just wondering if I could talk to your husband for a moment. Is he home?"

Over Mary's shoulder, Tessa saw a familiar form flit through the air. Chet Sanborn's spirit was there! She fought the urge to barrel over Mary to get to him, forcing her expression to stay relaxed and pleasant.

Mary glanced over her own shoulder and looked uneasy. "He's in his office catching up on a few things. He got behind with work while he was . . . detained."

"We heard the police let him go," Silas interjected. "That's good news. Do you know if they arrested someone else?"

Mary shook her head and stood aside to let them in. "No, the officer who released Mark said they didn't have any other leads."

They followed Mary through a cozy living room filled with worn furniture and discarded toys. Tessa continuously scanned for another sign of the ghost. They went down a short hall, past a bathroom, to a bedroom that had been converted to an office.

Mark sat behind a desk piled high with papers, a harried look on his face. His clothes and hair were rumpled.

Over his shoulder, Chet hovered.

Tessa could see glimpses of books on the shelves behind him through his half-transparent body. He glared at Tessa, shaking his spirit head from side to side. "I'm not ready."

She opened her mouth to reply but snapped it shut fast. Chet could speak without the others hearing him because they couldn't see spirits. But they'd hear her answer him clear as a bell—and think she was crazy.

Instead, she shot a quick glance back at the ghost before tearing her eyes away from him to focus on the live people in the room.

"Honey, this is the woman from the life insurance company and . . ." Mary shot a quizzical look at Silas.

"Her partner," he drawled, grinning. "Silas St. Onge."

Mark gave them a weary look. For a moment, recognition flitted across his face. "I've met so many people the past few days. I could swear you worked up at my dad's apartment complex."

"My, uh, my brother does."

Silas wasn't as good a liar as he'd claimed.

Mark shook his head. "Whatever. Nice to meet you. What can I help you with?"

Tessa itched to leap forward, open a way to the other side, and drag Chet Sanborn through it. But then she looked at his face. The glare was gone and in its place was an expression that looked almost begging. "Not yet. I'm not ready," he repeated, but this time, it sounded like a plea.

"Mr. Sanborn, I just need to get some information from you. As you can probably understand, your father's life insurance disbursement to you isn't valid if . . . well, if you killed him."

Mark nodded as if he expected this line of questioning.

"Can you please explain why you were released from jail?" Tessa couldn't keep her eyes from flitting to Chet periodically. She didn't trust the spirit to stay put.

"He didn't kill me," Chet argued.

"Shh!" Tessa admonished.

Mark looked confused. "What?"

She bit her lip. "I'm sorry. I, um, have some ear ringing that bothers me sometimes. Please . . . go ahead." She ignored Silas' gaze on her.

"Wouldn't it be easier to ask the cops?" He shook his head. "They cross-checked my cell phone records and location stamps against my digital time clock at work. It proved I was at the office when Dad died—just like I told them." He ran a hand over his face. Exhaustion radiated from him like heat waves from concrete in the summer.

"Told you so," Chet sneered.

Tessa pressed her lips together and forced herself not to glare at her mark. "Thanks for the information, Mark. And you'd be willing to sign something attesting to that once we have the lawyers draw it up, right?"

"Yeah, sure."

"You have to give me a little more time," Chet pleaded. "I have to make sure my son understands that I'm sorry."

"Sorry for what?"

Everyone looked at her, bewildered expressions on every face.

"I mean, I'm sorry for the inconvenience, Mr. Sanborn. I don't think I had enough coffee this morning." She laughed nervously.

Mark nodded. "I get that. And it's no sweat. I don't mind signing whatever I need to. At least I'm getting something back from the guy who had the nerve to steal from his own son."

"Your dad stole from you?" Silas sounded shocked.

"That's why I'm sorry," Chet whispered.

Mark nodded. "He gave me a Hank Aaron rookie card when I was a kid. It was my most prized possession. I thought it was the coolest thing ever. I thought it meant something—I thought it meant my dad loved me."

"I do love you," Chet said.

"Then, when he ran into some trouble with gambling debts, he stole it while he was over here eating my wife's famous lasagna." Mark's face twisted in disgust. "I guess he didn't love me after all. Or at least, he loved gambling more."

"I didn't realize he knew I'd taken it." Chet sounded miserable. "I never meant for him to know."

"I'm sure your dad was sorry about that," Tessa tried to help things along.

"I'm sorry about everything. Not just stealing the card but being a horrible father most of his life. I always thought the way to show him I loved him was to make lots of money and leave it to him. So he wouldn't have to work the way I did. But it turned out he would have rather had me spend time with him." He hung his ghostly head. "I returned the card. It's here—in the armoire."

Tessa's mind raced. How could she get Mark to find the card without revealing she could talk to spirits? She cleared her throat. "Your father took out an insurance policy on that card in your name. If it's not here in your home, then we'll need to file a report." Her heart pounded as she fought to keep from biting her lip. Silas was watching her carefully. Funny how overwhelming the urge was to nibble on it.

Mark's head jerked up. "It's not here. I checked a week ago."

"Maybe you should check again. Just in case? If it *is* missing, I'll need to draw up the paperwork." Tessa held her breath. It looked like Chet's spirit was holding his too, though she was the one who needed oxygen.

Mary moved to the armoire in the corner, opening one side. She dug around for a minute and then pulled out a cardboard box. "This is where your cards are, right, honey?"

"Yeah. But the rookie card isn't in there."

Mark squirmed in his seat and reached for the box. He pulled off the cover and gasped.

"Seriously? It's here. I don't believe it." He pulled out the card and set it on the desk. It was in a plastic protective case. Attached to the underside of the case, there was a sticky note. Mark scanned it. When he looked up, his eyes were filled with tears. "It's from Dad. It says he's sorry." He handed the note to his wife and wiped his eyes.

"Well, I'm glad you found it." Tessa turned to go, giving Chet a meaningful glance.

The spirit nodded. "That's all I needed."

Tessa stopped in the hallway and turned toward Mary. "Could I use your restroom before we go?"

"Sure." Mary gestured toward the room.

When Tessa closed herself in, Chet was already there.

"You've been a major problem for me, you know," she whispered as she waved a hand and the beam of light cut through the air.

"I'm sorry about that." Chet floated along the beam, his expression serene. "But sometimes you gamble and win. That's what I did."

"Wait a second," Tessa cried as Chet moved ahead quickly. "Who killed you?"

But he didn't answer. And in the next instant, he was gone.

Chapter 16

Tessa spent some time fighting the urge to go to her mom's house and gloat. She was having quite the day. Two spirits. It looked like reality was going to be fine. Now that Chet Sanborn had passed over, there was nothing much to fret about.

In the end, she figured Cheryl'd probably got some kind of notification from the higher-ups about it. And since she hadn't already called Tessa to congratulate her, it probably meant she was going to ignore the accomplishment altogether.

So, Tessa decided not to waste her time. She asked Silas to take her back to the apartment. After all, it was Sunday afternoon and Pepper was probably plotting something evil to get revenge for all the time she'd been forced to spend alone that week. Instead of a hair ball, Tessa may find herself stepping in something worse within the next few days.

She thought she should spend some quality time playing wand toy with the cat to avoid such a horrifying fate. And maybe after today's work, she could make things official and start paying Pepper's pet fee at the apartment.

But something niggled at her mind. Chet hadn't told Tessa who killed him. Of course, it really wasn't her problem anymore. She'd found her mark and sent him to the other side like she was supposed to do. Figuring out who'd killed him in the first place was the cops' puzzle to solve.

And yet . . .

"Aargh." She turned toward Silas, who had been uncharacteristically quiet.

"What? Is it talk like a pirate day?"

"No." She couldn't help but laugh. "It's not. But I need a favor."

"Another one?"

"Can you take me to the casino again?"

"I guess." He glanced at her before returning his eyes to the road and doing a legal U-turn after missing several spots to do one illegally.

"That was kind of strange back at Mark Sanborn's house . . ."

A tingle traveled up her spine. She concentrated hard on not biting her lower lip. "Was it? What do you mean?"

He shrugged. "Nothing, I guess." After thirty seconds of silence, he said, "I mean, it was just kind of crazy how you put that all together—about the card and it being back in the armoire. And then the note from Chet to his son. It just worked out so . . . so perfectly."

She recognized the strange tone in his voice. He knew something was up. Tessa worked to keep her tone even—and from biting her lip.

"Just a lucky guess on my part, really," she said. "I mean, he took out both policies through our agency, one on himself and one on the Hank Aaron card. I was doing my due diligence."

"Yeah. Lucky." He turned onto the highway, heading toward the casino. "And you're still not a very good liar by the way—even when you don't bite your lip."

Silence filled the cab for the rest of the ride. Tessa worked hard not to squirm. She didn't want to confirm Silas' suspicions that something wasn't right.

When he dropped her off in the casino's parking lot, he offered her a simple goodbye with no offer of waiting for her or coming along. She waved and hurried away, feeling his gaze on the back of her head.

Tessa marched onto the main floor of the casino, trying to ignore the smoke. She located a security camera and waved directly into it. She only had to wait for a few minutes before Horner showed up. He wasn't in the greeting mood.

"What do you want?" he growled.

"I want to talk to the boss."

"She doesn't have an appointment available. Call first next time." He turned his back to her.

"I need to talk to her about Chet Sanborn and the money he owed." She tried to sound mysterious, like she may know where the money was hidden. Then she held her breath, waiting to see if she'd hit the mark.

Horner stopped and turned back around, frowning.

"So. Can I please see Melinda?"

She couldn't tell if he was scowling or not—his normal expression was pretty much a constant sneer. But he finally jerked his head in a quick nod and led her through the blackjack room to the hallway that led to Melinda's fancy office. Tessa avoided eye contact with Ricardo as she passed through the blackjack room.

On the way back, Tessa wondered how Horner had gotten the scar on his face. Was it a childhood mishap or a grown man fight wound? Either way, it made him more menacing, that much was for sure.

He knocked on the door.

When Melinda's clear, strong voice beckoned them, Tessa didn't wait for an individual invitation. She brushed past the goon and marched up to the boss woman's desk.

"Ms. Randolph, you continually surprise me."

"Did Chet Sanborn really owe you money?" Tessa demanded. "Or did you owe it to him?"

Melinda's overly thin eyebrows migrated toward each other when she narrowed her eyes. Then she glanced over Tessa's shoulder. "You can go, Horner."

Once the door clicked behind him, Melinda sat back in her chair and steepled her fingers. "You're a nosy one, aren't you?"

Tessa didn't figure that required a reply. "Chet Sanborn didn't owe the casino money, did he?" she repeated. "I think you're trying to get the blackjack tournament prize money back."

"You do, do you?"

"Because you need it for your new house," Tessa added. *In for a penny . . .*

"My house? Really?" Melinda sighed. "No. We believed he was cheating. But the cameras weren't enough to get us the proof we needed."

"So, what, you thought he was counting cards or something?"

"Using a marked deck. Maddox and Horner went over to search his apartment for it." Melinda's tone and expression were cool—as though she ordered breaking and entering every day and her actions shouldn't be questioned.

"But how would he insert a marked deck into the game?" Tessa asked. "Doesn't the casino have safeguards in place for that sort of thing?"

What Tessa knew about casinos and gambling could fit on one sheet of paper if she wrote it down. It was nothing quite like Gloria's. But she'd watched a lot of movies.

Melinda's thin lips got thinner as her jaw clenched. Her next words came through gritted teeth. "The dealer would have to be involved too."

Ah. That makes sense.

If a casino employee was on the take, being blackmailed to use a marked deck, that would definitely be something the manager would want to root out and put a stop to. *But at the risk of her goons getting arrested for breaking and entering?*

"So, when your guys switched over to trying to find me because they saw me get arrested . . ."

"We thought you'd been involved somehow. Perhaps you'd disposed of the marked deck," Melinda finished.

It didn't sound like a story Melinda could make up on the fly. But an eerie thought skidded through Tessa's mind. What if Melinda hadn't ordered Chet's apartment searched? What if she'd been more sure of her suspicions that he was cheating the casino? Had she told the owners? What if this was the reason Chet had been killed?

Melinda's phone rang, and she picked it up. "Yes?" She listened for a moment. "No, that's not right. We need one branded car and twenty-eight golf carts for the charity tournament tomorrow." Another pause and then irritation flooded her features. She smacked the desk with her palm. "No! No, no, no. How many times do I have to tell you people that there will be fourteen teams of four. Fourteen fours. It's not hard."

Unable to shake the feeling that Melinda's actions had led to Sanborn's murder, Tessa took the opportunity to scoot out of the room and hurry down the hallway. Her thoughts raced as she tried to fit the puzzle pieces together. If someone connected to the casino had killed Chet, and they thought she was in on it too, then maybe they'd planned to kill her next.

Male voices drifted into the hallway from a side room. Something about the tone made Tessa pause and listen. "That's ridiculous! Chino's not going to go for that."

"She doesn't have a choice. This is a real mess, and if she wants to keep her fancy job and build her extravagant house, she'll let me handle it."

Tessa was sure that was Horner. He sounded venomous. She had a vision of him strangling Chet Sanborn and tossing him in the frigid water at the bottom of the pool. She hurried past the doorway, not glancing into the room. She didn't want Horner and whoever he was talking with to think she'd overheard anything.

Relief flooded her when she exited the hallway into the table games room. Ricardo was still at the blackjack table, but now, Gloria sat next to him, her chin resting on a fist. She wore dark maroon eye makeup and exactly matching lipstick, but her expression was forlorn.

Tessa started to cross the room to greet the other reaper, but then Ricardo surged out of his seat, fist pumped the air, and cheered, lunging forward to gather a big pile of chips into his arms. The others at the table grumbled and moaned. Gloria looked disinterested.

Someone brushed past Tessa, coming from behind her. It was Horner, approaching the blackjack table. But before he got there, the bulky man suddenly doubled over, clutching his abdomen.

Gloria sighed and got up, moving toward Melinda's goon. She waved a hand, and a beam of light appeared in the room. Horner's spirit rose from his body and hovered there, shock and confusion written all over the semi-transparent features.

Tessa moved next to Gloria. "Wow. I did *not* see that coming. Did he have a heart attack?"

"No." Gloria shook her head. "That man was poisoned."

Chapter 17

"That Horner guy—what a name." Cheryl shook her head. "That was supposed to be your assignment."

"It was?"

Cheryl nodded. "You lucked out, and I rearranged your schedule for Ellen Walker."

"Thanks for that." Tessa couldn't tell if her mother had meant it as a kind gesture or if she'd used it to ensure she stayed employed as a grim reaper. Either way, it had worked.

But her mother held her cards close, so to speak.

Tessa sank into the chair across from her mother's. "Hey, what do you know about that death, anyway? Gloria said it was poison. What kind of poison? Do you know who did it?"

Tessa had to admit—Horner had been her main suspect in Sanborn's death. Especially after she overheard his harsh words about Melinda, who had taken her turn as Tessa's main suspect too.

Cheryl rolled her eyes. "That isn't the kind of information we're given. You know that."

"I thought maybe you—"

"You think I have higher access. And you're right. I do. I suppose you think I should be thanking you for your little stunt?"

"For what?"

"For Chet Sanborn. You probably think you did good sending his spirit away like that—in a room full of people."

Chery looked livid, bringing back memories of the time Tessa had used her mother's crotchet needles to dig for worms in the back garden when she was seven. She'd simultaneously ruined the needles and the day lilies.

"Technically, he went in the bathroom."

"You know what I mean, Theresa."

Cheryl tapped her computer keyboard for a minute and then snapped, "I swear, Theresa. Between losing souls, not having your phone on, and insisting on driving that completely unreliable car around, I don't know how you expect to keep this job."

"Linda isn't unreliable. She's just picky about when she runs." Tessa batted her eyes and blinked slowly in an attempt to look innocent when her mother shot her a scornful look.

"You need to do better if you want to keep this job." Cheryl leaned forward, her expression suddenly probing with a hint of something else. *Insecurity?* "*Do* you want to keep this job?"

There it was.

Tessa thought of Ellen and her husband, reuniting in the next life. She thought of Chet, needing some time to make sure his son knew he was sorry for his less than stellar parenting before he moved on. And finally of Mark Sanborn, who would have the gift of spending the rest of his life knowing he'd meant something to his dad.

"I do," she said firmly. Tessa knew it was true. She did want to be a reaper.

Maybe she could even come to terms with what her dad had done for her—and with the hand her mother and the agency had in it.

Cheryl's face returned to its usual cool smoothness. "Fine. Then I suggest you start focusing on ways to improve your performance. You can start by giving up on the detective routine. That isn't what we do here."

"I'm not—"

"Your missing soul is safely across the veil now, so you can move on. Even this new guy—if it's connected—he's no concern of yours. Leave the murder mystery to the real detectives. The ones who get paid to solve it."

She focused on her computer screen, clearly dismissing her daughter.

Tessa started to head to her micro-office, but her mother's use of the word detective rang in her ears. She wasn't a detective, and she didn't get paid to be one, but the idea that a killer was loose in the community, still killing, was unsettling. Not only that, but Tessa also couldn't help but wonder if she may be next on the killer's hit list. After all, Maddox and Horner had come to her apartment. She wondered what her mother would think if she knew the whole story. But she was smarter than to tell her.

"You're right, Mom," she said when she was out the door. But she was thinking the opposite. Maybe she *should* act like a detective.

But what should her next step be? She spun around and made for her car instead, wracking her brain as she went. *What next?*

She knew Chet was a gambler. Not a great one, but he managed to get it right sometimes, like when he won the blackjack tournament. Except that had earned him suspicion of being a cheater.

Tessa got in the car and sat drumming her fingers on the wheel. Would Melinda have suspected any tournament winner of cheating? Probably not. Chet must have had a history of acting less than a hundred percent honestly.

Of course, Mark Sanborn already knew that about his father.

Tessa's brow furrowed. Why had Chet stolen the valuable baseball card from his son and then returned it? He'd told Tessa he never intended for Mark to find out the card was gone—which meant he'd needed the money for something but fully expected to be able to buy the card back in short order.

Maybe Chet had needed it for entry money for the tournament? Who could turn a baseball card into cash?

Outside almost every casino in the world sits a pawn shop. Mist River's was no different. She'd seen a pawn shop as she stared out the Silverado's window while Silas drove her to the casino. That would seem like an obvious choice of places for Chet to sell the baseball card.

She pulled out of the spot and pointed the car that way. When she got there, she frowned. The place was pretty run-down, with all the requisite neon signs in the big front windows declaring there to be jewelry, video games, sports paraphernalia, gold, and silver handled in the establishment. But the window itself didn't look like it had been cleaned in months.

Tessa took a deep breath before getting out of Linda to head into the shop. The bells over the door jangled, and an elderly man looked up from where he sat behind a long glass display case. He was perched on a stool, thumbing through a magazine that Tessa knew wasn't for the articles.

"What can I do you for?" His voice was higher than she'd expected.

"Hi," Tessa said, her voice sounding a little higher too. "I'm wondering if you can tell me anything about a specific transaction."

She approached the desk and peered inside. It was filled with engagement rings, watches, cuff links, and fancy coins. There were even some small metal statues and old-fashioned small appliances. Tessa spotted an open binder with baseball cards inserted in laminated sheets. "It was a Hank Aaron rookie card. Probably came in a week or two ago."

The man nodded, wispy gray hair floating around his face. "Yes, yes. I remember it. A man came in and pawned that card. Then he came back a few days later and paid me the money back." His face scrunched. "It was an odd thing, that. Another man came in a few days later with what looked like the same card. He said he bought it off another guy. But it was a fake."

Tessa's eyebrows shot up. "Seriously? How could you tell?"

He shrugged but puffed up self-importantly. "I've been doing this for a while, young lady. The ink on the second card wasn't right. Some of it even came off on my fingers."

"You're joking."

"I wish I was. It was quite obvious to me, but I had to prove it to the second man. He made me pull up a website on his newfangled phone and show him what it was supposed to look like." He chuckled, shaking his head. "You've never seen someone so angry before. Why, he swore up a blue streak, and I had to ask him to leave."

"What did this second guy look like?"

He pursed his lips as though thinking hard. "Well, let's see. He had on shorts and a gym-rat shirt. Fancy hair. Stupid looking shoes."

Ricardo. He had to mean Ricardo with his casino-typical outfit of a casino tank top and flip flops. Along with his fluffy toupee, the description matched him to a tee.

That was it. Chet must have double-crossed Ricardo, selling him a fake baseball card and refusing to give back the money.

"Thanks," she said. "I appreciate your time."

"No problem." He smiled. "Are you in the market for something nice for yourself? Maybe a fancy gold bracelet?" He pointed to a gaudy number with costume jewels on it.

"Oh, my. That's lovely," Tessa lied. "I'll have to pass. I've just started a new job, and I'm still catching up on bills. I'll keep it in mind for when I have some extra cash, though."

She didn't bite her lip, but she rambled. Another tell. She was making a list.

She left, planning to go back to the casino to confront Ricardo, but then her phone buzzed. She pulled it out and checked it. A text from her mother: Check your email. You have a new assignment.

Tessa clicked over to her email account and found the new message. She opened it, and her mouth fell open.

Her new target was Ricardo Vidale.

Chapter 18

The assignment was at the same golf club as her first—the same one her dad had frequented when he was alive. Tessa re-read the details three times before realizing it was going to happen at the golf tournament the casino was sponsoring. The one Melinda had mentioned the day before.

She glanced at the sky hopefully, but there was no way lightning would strike twice. Not on the same green in such short order.

Could it?

She scanned the document again and blinked after reading the cause of death.

Well, that's interesting.

Tessa gave herself plenty of time that morning to get there. But she breathed a sigh of relief when Linda started anyway.

"You've been so great lately," she gushed. "I'm definitely going to use some of my next paycheck to get you a tune-up. Especially if you get me to this assignment on time."

As she drove to the golf course, Tessa's mind raced. Ricardo must have been furious about Chet selling him a fake baseball card. It must've been worth a lot of money. Enough to kill over.

But why Horner? Tessa thought maybe he was getting close to fingering Ricardo for the crime. She knew criminals often worked in irrational and erratic ways. It troubled her how she'd drank a beer Ricardo bought her. She couldn't help but think their conversation might've led him down the path of harming Horner. She'd mentioned Melinda Chino. *Did I mention her goons too?* She shuddered. Ricardo could've poisoned her if she'd walked away from her drink for a moment.

And now it was her job to escort him to the other side.

Strange how, after everything that had happened over the past week, Ricardo would be taken out by a freak accident. Maybe there was such a thing as karma. She made a mental note to ask her mother or Gloria about that.

Wearing a blue polo and mid-thigh khaki shorts, Tessa managed to blend in with the crowd at the golf course. She snuck through the club onto the green again.

The area closest to the building was bustling. Tents were set up with tables under them, and the casino's logo was plastered on everything. There was a makeshift covered stage with a DJ, and golf carts came and went through the crowd.

Tessa threaded her way through the gaggle of golfers looking for Ricardo, but she couldn't spot him. Despite her timeliness, she started feeling nervous, like she might lose another soul. Ricardo's soul . . . *oi*. There was just no way she could let that happen. Cheryl would absolutely never, ever stop lecturing if she did.

She hurried onto the green, passing a shiny red car perched at the top of the hill. It was covered in magnetic signs proclaiming it to be the grand prize for the hole in one contest.

She scanned the valley below, one hand over her eyes to shield them from the sun's interfering glare. There were golfers spread out over the area, in pairs and foursomes, and she couldn't tell one from the other at that distance. She started down the hill.

It was really only chance that set her on the right path. At least, that's what it seemed like. Later, Tessa would wonder if it was part of her reaper powers—maybe some kind of radar. Whatever it was, when she crested a hill, she caught sight of Ricardo near a creek. The water hazard wound around the edge of the golf course. Next to a copse of trees.

Ricardo wasn't alone. Tessa recognized Maddox's man bun. As she approached, she could hear them talking. She slowed and crouched as low as possible, darting behind the men's golf carts to listen in.

Ricardo's face was red, as though he'd been walking the green in the sun. But when he spoke, it was clear the extra coloring was from anger. "I can't be part of it anymore," he said. "It was one thing when Chet was here. We worked together and it took the pressure off. But now he's gone, thanks to you."

"What are you saying?" Maddox asked.

"You know what I'm saying—I'm saying I'm out."

Tessa was shocked. Had the two men been working together all along? And what part did Chet Sanborn play?

"Chet shouldn't have crossed me," Maddox snarled. The expression looked strange on his usually placid face. "He should've given me the money I asked for—not try to play me with that false card."

"What choice did he have?" Ricardo asked. "When you make a deal, it's set in stone. You can't keep changing the terms like you do. Chet needed that money to get the real card back."

"They were my terms to change. He was still making enough on that deal and you know it."

Ricardo wavered, conceding defeat. "Fair enough."

"You aren't going to make the same mistake Chet did, are you?"

"I'm not." Ricardo paled a bit and took a step back. "But I want to know one thing—what did Horner do to set you off?"

Maddox's mouth twisted into a smirk. "He figured out I offed Chet. He was going to tell Melinda. And she would've called the police for sure."

"I'm surprised they haven't connected the dots."

His face twisted in derision. "They won't. All trails lead to Melinda Chino. She doesn't have the spine for this kind of business. She wants the profit but doesn't want to do what's necessary. If I hadn't gotten rid of Chet, he'd have kept finding ways to cheat the casino."

"So, she doesn't know what you did? To Chet or Horner?" Ricardo's voice wasn't as strong as before.

Maddox spat on the ground. "She doesn't have a clue. She just knows the money is safe. I'm the brains and the brawn of our partnership."

"And what am I? The fall guy?" Ricardo shook his head. "You can't blackmail me anymore. If I get caught—if the cops catch me cheating, I'll go to jail, and you won't say a word to help me out."

"That's the risk you take."

"Chet and I did it for the money, but it's too hot now. It's not worth it anymore. I'm out." He started to walk away from Maddox. "I'm going to get a burger in the club. Then I'm going home. You won't see me at the casino anymore. Get yourself a new blackjack plant."

Maddox rushed toward the golf cart, pulling out a club. "Eating animal flesh is disgusting," he said, raising the club over his head.

Tessa straightened to her full height and crossed her arms.

Seeing her appear seemingly out of nowhere, Maddox faltered. "What are you doing here?"

"Get out of here, Ricardo," Tessa said, jerking her head toward the club building. "Go call the police."

Ricardo didn't move.

"Did you hear all that?" Maddox asked, staring hard at Tessa.

"I did." Tessa kept her gaze on Maddox even as she saw movement over his shoulder. Something was coming from the top of the hill. "I heard everything. You're a murderer. A vegan, Birkenstock-wearing, man-bun sporting murderer, which is weird, but still."

Maddox raised the club again. He rushed toward Tessa. She waited as long as possible. Then, she leaped to the side, yanking Ricardo with her by the arm.

She didn't know if someone had left the shiny red car in neutral or if they just didn't set the emergency brake when they parked the car at an angle at the top of the hill. Either way, it gained speed as it careened down the hill and smashed into Maddox, carrying his body with it until it landed nose-first in the water hazard.

Ricardo shouted. He ran up the hill, arms pumping wildly. He only made it halfway before he collapsed, panting and wailing about how sorry he was. How he'd never do anything illegal again if the angry spirits would just let him live. His toupee lurched to the side, so it drooped low over his right ear.

Maddox's spirit rose out of the creek and stared in disbelief at the tangled pile of metal. He jerked his head toward Tessa, a question on his face. "Did you just kill me?"

She shook her head. "Nope. I facilitated an exchange. A soul for a soul." She shrugged. "Sometimes, the universe just gets it wrong."

And sometimes a grim reaper has to take matters into her own hands.

Tessa flicked her wrist, watching as a beam of light shot down from the sky. "Time to go, Maddox."

For the first time, he looked uneasy. He peered into the light. "Wh . . . where am I going?"

She shrugged. "I have no idea. That's not my department."

Chapter 19

Silas handed her the keys to Linda with an adorable wink and a dimple-revealing grin. "She's as good as new."

Tessa raised one eyebrow in suspicion. "New? Really?"

He chuckled. "Okay, she's as good as a thirty-year-old car can be."

She nodded once. "Perfect. That's just how I like her. Thanks for the tune-up. I know you don't have a lot of extra time to be doing work for free."

"It's no sweat." Silas brushed his brow with a forearm, proving it did cost a bit of sweat. He stuffed his hands in his pockets and looked at his feet. "And you're right about the time. It's crazy around this place. But I fit things in when it's important to me."

"Linda's important to you?"

He smiled. "I just don't want this bucket of rust leaving you on the side of the road."

That brought up the memory of Frank leaving her on the side of the highway one night. She'd never shake the long, dusty walk home.

What a jerk.

"Thanks. I don't want that either." She opened Linda's driver's side door and gasped in surprise. "It doesn't squeak anymore!"

"The magic of grease. I changed out a couple of rusty bolts for you too. And a headlight."

"I must owe you more money." She'd insisted that Silas let her at least buy the parts, even though the service was free.

"Nah." He shook his head. "I didn't use enough WD-40 to cost you anything."

"I could really pay you with my next paycheck." She got in the car and fired it up. It sounded great. Better than great. "She sounds like a new girl."

The dimples popped from his cheek.

"Thanks again!" Tessa reached for the gear shifter to put Linda in reverse but a knock on the window stopped her. She rolled down the window and gave Silas a questioning look.

"One more thing," Silas said.

"So, I do owe you money, don't I!"

He shook his head, still smiling. "I occasionally take a few minutes out to eat dinner. Would you maybe want to go with me sometime?" He kicked at the asphalt. "You know, when *you* have time. Your new job seems to have odd hours."

Tessa's pulse raced. She took a breath in an attempt to get it to settle down. "I think I'd like that, but . . ."

"But?"

"I'm paying," she said proudly. "It's the least I could do." She knew that was true, but she'd have to work it out with her bank account.

"Sounds good." He grinned widely, nodded, and headed for the building.

Tessa rolled up the window and gave a little squeal. Then she thought about how dating and then breaking up with Frank had cost her a job. Maybe dating her landlord would risk her apartment? At the very least, she'd have to see him every day. Maybe it wasn't such a good idea.

But those thoughts only took a minute to fade away. She didn't care. He was cute, and he wanted to take her out. It was time she enjoyed herself. After all, what would her dad think?

She sang all the way to the agency. It felt like her feet never touched the ground as she danced inside. She went directly to her mother's office.

Cheryl glanced up from the computer and then raised her eyebrows. "Why so cheerful? Did the order for my demise come in?"

"Mom!"

Cheryl smirked at her grim joke.

Tessa shrugged and leaned on the door frame. "I don't know. It's a nice day."

"Well, don't get too excited. You have two assignments today. If you manage to get to them both on time—and not lose any souls—you can call it a nice day." She went back to tapping on the keyboard.

Tessa entered the office, closing the door behind her. That earned her another questioning glance from her mother.

Tessa sat across the desk from her. "How often does it happen?"

"How often does what happen?" Cheryl's fingers hovered over the keyboard.

"You know—someone taking another person's place."

Cheryl sighed and put her hands in her lap. She eyed the door. "Not often. It's been known to happen by accident on occasion, but usually, it's a decision made by the reaper on duty."

"And it's allowed?"

"It causes a lot of red tape. What you did yesterday will wind up being years of paperwork. That's my job."

"So, I shouldn't have done it?"

A small smile flitted over Cheryl's lips, but it disappeared as fast as it came. "I didn't say that," she said softly. "But Ricardo may wish you'd done something else. He's probably going to spend a lot of time in jail."

"Melinda was hopping mad. I'm sure she'll press charges." The casino boss had been in the golf club when everything went down. Everything was madness. An ambulance, fire trucks, and police officers had descended on the country club in short order.

When Tessa got back from escorting Maddox across the veil, she'd made sure Ricardo came clean on the whole thing with a threat of taking him next.

Both women chuckled.

"So, I get to keep my job?" Tessa tipped her head and studied her mother's features.

"For now." Cheryl nodded. "In fact, you've earned yourself a spot at the annual conference in Florida. You and Gloria can go together and share a hotel room."

"Wait. There's a reaper conference once a year? In Florida?"

"There is. And it's not always in Florida. It's usually somewhere tropical. Or Vegas." Cheryl shuddered. "I'm not going to be able to get away for it this year. So, you and Gloria will represent our office."

For some reason, the idea of a bunch of reapers sitting in a conference room watching PowerPoint slideshows made Tessa want to belly laugh. But the idea of an all-expenses-paid getaway was a welcome one.

"The company pays for this?" Tessa asked.

"We do." Cheryl paused and squinted at Tessa. "And I'll expect you both to behave and comport yourselves with dignity." Her tone held a note of warning that Tessa was quite familiar with. She'd heard it every time she went out with her friends as a teenager.

"I'll try." She got up to leave and turned at the door. "I can't speak for Gloria, though. She seems a little wild." Tessa winked.

"Theresa." Cheryl's voice was soft and gentle. "One more thing."

Tessa froze. Another one more thing. And this one didn't sound as good as Silas' offer. Something was strange about her mother's tone of voice. Tessa didn't dare make eye contact. Not even to correct her use of the long form of her name.

"I'm sorry about your dad," Cheryl said. "I knew what he was going to do that day. He didn't say it outright, but I knew. And I didn't stop him. I didn't know what to do."

"Mom, it's—"

"I should have stopped him." Cheryl's voice broke. "But . . . but I didn't want to lose either of you. I wish I had my own Maddox."

Tessa turned around slowly, seeing tears skid down her mother's cheeks.

"Actually, I do know what I should have done. I shouldn't have let him take your place. I should have done it. And I regret every day that I didn't." She wiped her cheek, chin quivering.

Feeling a wave of empathy, Tessa rushed forward. She knelt in front of Cheryl and squeezed her hand. "No, don't say that, Mom. I'm so glad you're here."

Cheryl met Tessa's gaze and smiled. Something released inside Tessa. She realized she'd been angry with her mother. Mad that she hadn't somehow found a way to save Michael Randolph. But as she held her mom's hand, she felt a wave of forgiveness. It wasn't Cheryl's fault.

With one last squeeze, Tessa stood. "I'd better go. I don't want to be late for my assignment."

"Definitely not." Cheryl hiccupped.

"Yeah. My boss is a real dragon lady." She winked and left the office, her mother's laugh following her out.

When Tessa got outside, she lowered the sunglasses from the top of her head to her face and turned toward the sun, feeling happy. It was almost the best season in Mist River, Michigan. Summer. She had a date with a cutie landlord. Her junker car was running great. And she had a new job she was good at. And not just a job that anyone could do, but a real career.

She smiled widely and looked to the sky, sending her dad a silent thank you. She was sure he had something to do with helping her life get straightened out.

She laughed at the irony as she headed toward Linda.

Who knew being a grim reaper would be her calling?

Also By Christine Zane Thomas

Witching Hour starring 40 year old witch Constance Campbell

Book 1: Midlife Curses[1]

Book 2: Never Been Hexed[2]

Book 3: Must Love Charms[3]

Book 4: You've Got Spells[4]

Tessa Randolph Cozy Mysteries written with Paula Lester

Grim and Bear It[5]

The Scythe's Secrets[6]

Reap What She Sows[7]

Foodie File Mysteries starring Allie Treadwell

The Salty Taste of Murder[8]

A Choice Cocktail of Death[9]

A Juicy Morsel of Jealousy[10]

The Bitter Bite of Betrayal[11]

---

1. https://alsoby.me/r/amazon/B085GJLYCF?fc=us&ds=1

2. https://alsoby.me/r/amazon/B085J3DF8S?fc=us&ds=1

3. https://alsoby.me/r/amazon/B086R3HVRQ?fc=us&ds=1

4. https://alsoby.me/r/amazon/B086R8HMKK?fc=us&ds=1

5. https://alsoby.me/r/amazon/B085X2Q4LV?fc=us&ds=1

6. https://alsoby.me/r/amazon/B085X3L55M?fc=us&ds=1

7. https://alsoby.me/r/amazon/B085X2R3XL?fc=us&ds=1

8. https://alsoby.me/r/amazon/B07HGCRRSX?fc=us&ds=1

9. https://alsoby.me/r/amazon/B07J2VN5RY?fc=us&ds=1

10. https://alsoby.me/r/amazon/B07JN828F8?fc=us&ds=1

11. https://alsoby.me/r/amazon/B07N6MYF6Z?fc=us&ds=1

Comics and Coffee Case Files starring Kirby Jackson and Gambit

Book 1: Marvels, Mochas, and Murder[12]
Book 2: Lattes and Lies[13]
Book 3: Cold Brew Catastrophe[14]
Book 4: Decaf Deceit[15]

---

12.   https://alsoby.me/r/amazon/B07J2TFBCB?fc=us&ds=1

13.   https://alsoby.me/r/amazon/B07MRCJ56R?fc=us&ds=1

14.   https://alsoby.me/r/amazon/B07NKTHCDG?fc=us&ds=1

15.   https://alsoby.me/r/amazon/B07SYC5MV5?fc=us&ds=1

About Christine Zane Thomas

Christine Zane Thomas is the pen name of a husband and wife team. A shared love of mystery and sleuths spurred the creation of their own mysterious writer alter-ego.

While not writing, they can be found in northwest Florida with their two children, their dachshund Queenie, and schnauzer Tinker Bell. When not at home, their love of food takes them all around the South. Sometimes they sprinkle in a trip to Disney World. Food and Wine is their favorite season.

About Paula Lester

Sign up for Paula's newsletter to receive information on book releases, other fun information, book recommendations, promos, and more: https://sendfox.com/lp/10q2rm
You can see all of Paula's books at: www.paulalester.com

***

Works by Paula Lester:

***

**Beachside Books Magical Cozy Mysteries
(Co-Authored with Lisa B. Thomas)**
Pasta, Pirates and Poison
Apples, Actors and Axes
Grits, Gamblers and Grudges
Candy, Carpenters and Candlesticks
Meatballs, Mistletoe and Murder
Honey, Hearts and Homicide

***

**Crystal Springs Cozy Witch Mysteries
(Co-Authored with M.E. Harmon)**
Dead Witch Talking (prequel novella)
A Witch Too Late
A Witch Too Hot
A Witch Too Bright
A Witch Too Dead

A Witch Too Frozen
A Witch Too Soon

***

Isles of Mer Cozy Witch Mysteries
(Co-Authored with M.E. Harmon)

Sandy Seances
Seaside Spells
Bewitched Breakers

***

Cruise Ship Cozy Mysteries
(Co-Authored with M.E. Harmon)

Cruising for a Bruising
Angling for a Strangling
Yearning for a Burning

***

Sunnyside Retired Witches Community Mysteries

Ghostly Trails
A Bottle Full of Djinn
Loony Town
Mummy Issues
Clairvoyant Clues
Boss Blues
Engine Repairs
Wedding Whack
Turnabout Time

***

Sunnyside Magical Bakery Cozy Mysteries
Sugar Skulls and Suspects
Tea Tarts and Trespassers
Mint Macarons and Murderers

***

Superior Bay Witch Doctor Mysteries
Witch Doggone Killer?
The Affairs of Witches
Witch Way Out?

***

Unfamiliar Magic Mysteries
Infurior Magic

***

Tessa Randolph Grim Reaper Cozy Mysteries
(Co-Authored with Christine Zane Thomas)
Grim and Bear It
The Scythe's Secrets
Reap What She Sows

www.ingramcontent.com/pod-product-compliance
Lightning Source LLC
Chambersburg PA
CBHW021011180726
47993CB00019B/2219